SAV

A SCI-FI ROMANCE
J.M. LINK

Copyright © February 2018, J.M. Link
All rights reserved.
Except for brief quotes used in reviews, no part of this book may be reproduced or transmitted in any form or by any means without express written consent from the author.

In case you need telling, *Saving Askara* is a work of fiction and any resemblance to real people, places, events and/or things is purely coincidental...or perhaps a slip from J.M.'s rebellious subconscious. Who knows what the heck goes on in there.

Cover design by Maria Spada
Edits by Aquila Editing

To my ever-supportive mother, who taught me what it was to dream. And that finding your passion in life is just as important as paying the bills.

To my wonderful husband and partner, who helps keep me grounded through all my whimsical ramblings.

I love you, sweetheart.

To my brother: a true kindred spirit and fellow adventurer, star-gazer and all-around Renaissance man.

Heartfelt thanks to my sister (in-law)/ "editor," for her early guidance.

And lastly, to all my friends and family who have been so incredibly supportive in every way. Thank you so much.

Love much. Laugh often. Dream big.

Chapter One

Dr. Victoria Davis fidgeted nervously as she felt the shuttle dock with the south gate of the *Amendment*. It was the largest Earth-orbiting maintenance station, though the occupant ship was anything but terrestrial.

Her heart pounded, and her throat was dry as she tried to ignore the uneasy ache in her stomach. *I can't believe it. I can't believe this is happening.*

The morning had seemed to start out normal enough. She'd barely started her shift when she received an emergency page from her supervisor, Dale Johnson.

"And it begins," she'd sighed, a little peeved she couldn't even shove down some breakfast before the daily mayhem began. She sent a quick text to her best friend that she wouldn't be able to make it to the cafe for their usual grunting over coffee, since she *so* wasn't a morning person.

Liv was the closest thing Tori had to family since her parents had died. They'd met in med school, but Liv had dropped out to ultimately pursue counseling, deciding the stress and demands of being a doctor weren't worth it. *Sometimes she's absolutely right,* Tori thought. Her best friend's reply was instant.

DIDN'T YOU CATCH THE EMERGENCY BROADCAST??!!!

Tori frowned. What emergency broadcast? Come to think of it, something did seem off, she realized, looking around. The halls were unusually empty, and the few staff she did glimpse seemed tense and hurried.

No, pulled a double. Slept at the Clinic... Why? What's going on??

She'd barely sent the response when her ear-comm went off. "Ugh, come on," she muttered before answering. "Davis here."

"*Where* the hell are you?! I need you here *now*, as in five minutes ago!" a male voice barked.

Tori frowned, a little taken aback. "Jesus, Dale, I'm on my way," she said, picking up the pace. "I only just got your page; what do we have?" She'd never heard him so worked up. Blunt and demanding, yes. But as Chief of Medicine aboard the *Phoenix,* the most advanced orbiting passenger ship, literally the size of a small city, with a fully staffed, hospital-sized Med Ward, Johnson was always cool, calm and collected, no matter what the situation.

There was nothing but silence, and for a moment she thought he'd disconnected.

"You're kidding." He sounded stunned, another first. "You haven't heard?"

"Heard what? What's going on?" she repeated, getting a little annoyed.

Tori looked down just as Liv's reply came through, and stopped in her tracks. *This must be a joke,* she thought, blinking at the clip Liv had forwarded.

Dale's voice was in her ear, but she stood frozen, trying to mentally process what she was seeing.

Holy Hell. It's actually happening...

The mind-shattering discovery that extraterrestrial life existed was made quite some time ago and had since been accepted as common knowledge. That life had been in the form of small bacteria-like microbes on the surfaces of moons like Titan and Europa, but the point was made nonetheless; life outside of Earth was possible and did exist. The real game-changer, though, had happened relatively recently, when an advanced new probe sent into deep space had detected a signal. A signal, scientists argued, that was not naturally occurring and not man-made.

The implications had rocked the world. But no matter how hard they tried, experts hadn't been able to crack its meaning, or origin, and most people didn't know whether to believe it or not. Religious groups denied it as a hoax, as did some governments. As a space enthusiast, Tori was more than excited at the possibilities, but those weren't reality, and life went on. The hype eventually died down, but there was no doubting that things had never been the same since.

Faced with potential proof that humans weren't the only intelligent beings in the universe, most developed nations had begun to invest heavily in technology and space travel to prepare for, maybe not the inevitable, but the probable. The world of only fifty years before seemed primitive in comparison, and one liked to think the race, as a whole, had mentally matured to some degree. It was pretty damn amazing what people could accomplish when they got their heads out of their asses and started working together.

No one could deny, however, what lay beneath it all... Fear of whatever was out there, what it was capable of.

"Davis!" Dale's authoritative tone broke through her stupor. "Did you understand *any* of what I just said?"

Tori's heart pounded, and her mind reeled. He let loose a vicious curse, another rare occurrence.

"Never mind, just get your butt down here ASAP. I'll brief you then. We have a shuttle leaving in twenty and you need to be on it."

So here she was, about to come face to face with extraterrestrials.

Once she got over the initial shock, or at least acted with-it enough to seem so, she'd been quickly briefed and loaded onto the transport shuttle. As head of emergency medicine on a space-faring vessel, Tori was used to functioning under extreme stress, keeping a cool head no matter what she was up against...but boy, was this pushing it.

In a few short minutes, they'd be ushered through the shuttle doors, onto the *Amendment* and directly to the station's Med Ward. An image of the holo-pics she'd seen surfaced again, and Tori had to reach deep to steel her resolve.

Demons. That's what they were calling them, and she could understand why. They had dark, graphite-colored skin, sharp teeth, pointed ears, and large, almost cat-like eyes. Plus, they were big—standing, on average, well over six feet.

First impressions? They were terrifying. Which is why as she looked around the shuttle's cabin, she was grateful for the military guards who would be escorting them.

There were four other doctors besides herself, the *Phoenix* being the only vessel in the vicinity with sufficient, highly trained medical personnel to spare for such an operation. Tori recognized Hodges, Menez and Matthews. *Great.*

Matthews was a neurologist/neurosurgeon and the biggest prick Tori had ever met. The man took the term "God complex" to a whole new level. She always hated having to deal with him for consults—he treated everyone, even colleagues, like they were total morons. Not a great first impression for mankind, in her opinion.

She glanced over to catch the gray-eyed stare of Delia Brooks, one of the ship's anesthesiologists, and the only other woman on the shuttle. The petite blonde looked about as calm as Tori felt, so she gave her a tight, reassuring smile before facing forward again. She swallowed hard, mouth feeling like cotton, and clenched her hands in her lap to stop their trembling. *Just breathe.*

"You're not gonna pass out on me, are ya, Doc?" a deep voice rumbled near her ear. "You look awful pale."

Her eyes flew open to catch the concerned gaze of the guard sitting next to her. He'd introduced himself earlier, but Tori barely remembered, everything was a blur. He seemed nice enough, and in any other circumstance she might have found his warm brown eyes and muscular six foot...two? frame attractive, but not today.

"It's Tori, and I'm fine. Just missed breakfast...though I suppose that's a good thing," she muttered, thinking there was no way she would have kept it down right now.

"All right everybody, listen up." Their team lead stood, commanding everyone's attention. He was dressed in the same black uniform as the man next to her, with weapons clearly visible, strapped to both thighs, and a protective vest.

"Just to reiterate, when the shuttle doors open you'll be led to Decon, then on to the Med Ward. You're to report to Ambassador Wells; he'll fill you in and direct you to where you're needed. Remember, the *Amendment* is a repair station, not a first-class luxury cruiser, so you won't have access to the kind of advanced equipment you're used to." He paused, frowning slightly. "Also remember, they're going to be able to understand you just fine. We suspect some sort of advanced neural interface, but they're able to speak all languages fluently." He paused again, eyeing them each pointedly. "You're representing the human race, boys and girls. Let's act accordingly."

The guy sitting next to her leaned closer. "I've been around them since they arrived. Take some getting used to," he said in a low voice. "But don't worry." He winked. "You'll have plenty of us looking out for you."

Tori blinked.

Awesome, I get to deal with flirty Captain America, she thought, right before they all began to exit the shuttle. At least it kept her mind somewhat distracted from what she was about to face.

Chapter Two

"Whatever you need, we'll do our best to help you."

Aderus stared down at the *hu-man* ambassador. The top of the male's head came to his shoulders, though he stood taller than the rest. He heard a quiver in his voice, noticed how the diplomat couldn't seem to hold his gaze for very long without glancing away. He studied his pale skin and thin, willowy frame, and judged the human as barely half his weight. Was it his size or the dark tone of his skin that the Earthling found disturbing? Probably both.

Their small army of escorts all eyed him strangely. His nose twitched; the air was heavy with a sharp scent. Fear, if their rapidly beating hearts were any indication. He supposed his kind would seem frightening to them, though the one speaking tried harder to hide it.

Aderus held back a hiss of frustration. The male spoke incessantly. It was one thing he'd noted about humans so far. They talked. A lot. His kind communicated primarily via their other senses. When he did answer a question, it was concise and sufficient. The human would look at him expectantly, then begin rambling again.

His upper lip twitched. Flashing his teeth in annoyance would likely not help how they viewed them so far.

Instead he diverted his attention to the ship around them, discreetly observing as much as he could. To say he was reluctant to appeal to this isolated little world for help would be an understatement. They simply had no choice. He and the others were lucky to have survived and he knew he should be grateful.

Instead he felt frustration, anger, and yes, fear.

They had been hurtling through Askara's atmosphere, a contingent of *Maekhur* vessels upon them. He was certain they wouldn't survive when they were forced to *ssvold* while still in the grip of the planet's atmosphere. But dying in a fight for freedom was better than the alternative.

Who should make him feel that dreaded emotion now but the pale-skinned, thinly beings before him. Aderus's sharp gold eyes flicked back to the ambassador. He didn't fear any one Earther in particular. It was being at the mercy of their race, as a whole, and how they would choose to act that made him anxious. He and the others had survived great odds only to be thrust into an even more impossible situation.

One they dreaded with all their being—what was called a *Dekhaveep* or "Awakening."

It was something his kind never did, as indoctrinating a new race was incredibly dangerous. Most were not accepting of other-worlders, especially when they appeared as threatening as his kind obviously did to the humans. Their numbers were few, the advantage of their technology negated by the condition of their ship. Survival now depended on one thing. Diplomacy.

Aderus clicked his claws, agitated. He struggled mightily with the idea. They were not a social species. In fact, most other races found them too challenging to deal with and so tended to shy away. Though there were other reasons... How the others had volunteered him for this was beyond him. Their predicament was already making it hard to control his impulses.

They had just traded one desperate situation for another.

A large port view automatically drew his gaze over the top of the ambassador's head. *Earth.* The small blue planet, so different from his home yet beautiful in its own way, he supposed. Blindingly bright due to a nearby yellow *sun*, it was hot, lush, and covered in deep blue oceans with swirling white clouds. In contrast, Askara orbited a much larger gaseous planet, *Kharhisshna*. The light from their red dwarf star was a dim glow in comparison, their home world dark and cool.

His race, children of their mother world just as humans were children of Earth; it made him long for home.

He directed his gaze back to the ambassador, who seemed to fidget nervously under his scrutiny. Aderus couldn't help staring at the similarities they shared with this species, despite their differences. Of course, the naïve Earthers were completely focused on the latter.

He knew they called them "Demon," and understood it was not an endearing name. Such mythical creatures were feared and often respected, however. Hopefully, it would afford them a measure of the same. Besides, he and the others had found images of the creatures quite appealing. So, they had embraced the designation, even choosing Demon-like names, as humans did not possess the complex vocal cords necessary to pronounce their natural names.

The air suddenly shifted, and Aderus tensed. The mention of propulsion systems in the next instant explained it. The male kept speaking, watching him with a keen intensity while Aderus averted his gaze.

Here was what he had been waiting for. Despite all they had said, he knew what they would want in exchange for their seemingly gratis aid. It was what all less advanced races wanted when they encountered one more advanced.

But it would not happen.

Their situation was precarious; they would not give up their only leverage. This contact was based on necessity, not a willingness to interact and/or share knowledge. The few who made it through unharmed were already working diligently. Getting the vessel repaired and operational was their one primary directive, because every moment here was a moment wasted fighting for the very survival of their species.

"We have a team of medical specialists arriving at any moment to assist with—" the ambassador continued, but Aderus cut him off, nostrils flaring. Did this presumptuous being really believe it would be so easy to get what he wanted?

"We did not request specialists."

His tone must have been more forceful than he realized because the Earther took two steps back. "We need only supplies," he tried again.

"Uh, my apologies," the human official said, clearing his throat. "There must have been a miscommunication."

Aderus watched as the male's eyes darted to something behind him and back. "A-are you certain your man wouldn't like some assistance from our doctors? They're the absolute best at what they do, and from what I understand, the basics of your biology aren't that much different from our own."

The diplomat couldn't be more wrong, though Aderus knew it was better he be allowed to think so. Considering the vast diversity of life in the universe, their physical forms and features *were* remarkably similar. But physiology was another matter entirely.

***

Just my luck. Tori swallowed, trying for even, measured breaths as she followed an armed escort through several hallways and airlocks to the *Amendment's* Med Ward. It was located on the same level as the main docking gate, which made sense. It wasn't uncommon for incoming vessels in need of repair to have injured passengers or crew.

A Dr. Evans had met them all at Decon, and while the others had been held back for a quick briefing on protocol, she, being the emergency medicine specialist, was sent ahead to assist. She hadn't even been able to appreciate the look of jealous disdain from a beady-eyed Matthews because at this moment, she really wished their roles were reversed.

They rounded another corner and Tori almost stumbled as she realized what was filling the hallway a mere thirty feet in front of her. Her eyes went wide, her heart pounded, and time seemed to slow. It was an indescribable feeling. Intense didn't even come close.

She was staring at her first real live alien. *Extraterrestrial*, she corrected herself.

The male was tall—at least she assumed it was a he. Over six feet, she guessed. Not entirely uncommon, but to someone only five four, it was big. His overall bone structure, however, was...different. Solid, gracefully built. But not human looking. He wore a form-fitting black uniform, the material unlike anything she'd ever seen. It seemed to reflect the light so that while Tori could see his general shape, it was hard to make out details.

He stood with his back to her. Even at this distance Tori could see what looked like thick, textured braids covered his head. She was focusing on his ears when movement to the right drew her attention.

She vaguely recognized the dark-haired, middle-aged man as Ambassador Wells, having seen him a few times in passing aboard the *Phoenix*. The man's light brown eyes locked on her, his expression one of unease.

"...At any rate, may I introduce Dr. Victoria Davis," she heard him say, gesturing to her as she approached on legs that felt like jelly.

The Demon turned then, and Tori's breath caught as a pair of the most amazing golden eyes locked on her. Only a few feet from the large alien now, she observed they were a bright molten color, ringed with black. Inky lines bled into the centers, pointing toward slightly elongated pupils. His irises were also huge, covering most of the eye, but for a little gray that was visible around the edges when they moved. They were absolutely striking, especially in contrast to his dark skin. It was difficult, but she forced her gaze away from them to take in the rest of his features.

His "nose" was more of a snout, a wide bridge with a flat bone that appeared to run all the way to the tip. She noted his more pronounced brow, cheekbones, and jaw, and realized that the holo-pics she'd seen did his kind little justice. The picture one of them painted in person was entirely different. Yes, he was chilling. But equally mesmerizing.

Someone was trying to get her attention and Tori pulled her gaze away to meet the ambassador's impatient expression.

"Dr. Davis is the head of emergency medicine aboard the *Phoenix*, our most advanced passenger vessel," he said after clearing his throat.

"Um, yes. Sorry," she managed when she finally regained the power of speech, dazedly extending her hand in greeting.

The Demon's gaze dropped. It took Tori several moments to realize he wasn't responding.

Wells leaned over to whisper in her ear and a blush exploded up her neck and across her cheeks. She went to pull back, but not before something brushed her hand. It had to be the shortest handshake in human history, and Tori struggled to lock down the sensation. His palm had felt rough, but some skin she'd grazed with her fingertips had been smooth, almost rubbery. His thumb was nearly the length of his other fingers, which looked like they had an additional joint compared to hers. They were tipped with hooked black claws. She felt her heart speed up again and cleared her throat before glancing up at him.

"It's very nice to meet you…uh, I-I'm so sorry, I don't think I caught your name."

They had probably said it while she'd been gawking like a moron. Gods, she felt like such a spaz! But in her defense, there weren't many people who wouldn't in this situation.

"Aderus," he replied in what she could only describe as an almost dissonant voice, and little goose bumps raced up her arms. His vocal cords were two-toned, like an organ.

"Aderus," she repeated, liking the name, though she knew it was not his own. "Please, call me Tori." She'd never liked the "doctor" title. In her mind, it automatically put up a wall that, if anything, made her job more difficult.

He didn't respond except to stare, and she felt a chill run up her spine. Everything about him—his appearance, the way he seemed to move, his stare—was animalistic. From what she could tell, it was just their nature.

"I must return to the others," he said, looking to the ambassador now.

Tori blinked as the large Demon turned dismissively to walk back down the corridor, leaving Wells beside her, stuttering in a search for words.

Wait. All that buildup, and they didn't want her help?

Was it something I said? Something I did? Maybe she'd insulted him in some way.

Her eyes happened to catch on his arm as he turned away, and by some insanely stupid impulse, she reached out. Big mistake. The tips of her fingers barely made contact, but the large alien instantly tensed and turned on her with what sounded like a deep-throated hiss, his thin upper lip curling to reveal *two* rows of sharp, silvery teeth. The movement was so abrupt that it pulled her forward and off balance for a moment. They were inches apart, with him towering over her, and Tori felt all the color drain from her face. She heard the guards behind her react and thought quickly, desperate to defuse the situation.

"I-I'm sorry!" she said, pulling back. "I meant no offense. I just saw that, you're wounded," she explained, looking to the deep gashes on his forearm, where the uniform didn't cover. He looked down then, as if just noticing the lacerations. *How did he not feel that? It looked painful as hell.* She licked her lips, his intense eyes following the gesture.

"Please, let me treat them for you. It's why I'm here."

Chapter Three

Aderus studied the female as she prepared to tend his arm. He took note of the others standing just outside, then looked back at *Tori,* as she'd told him to call her. He'd kept a good distance from their ambassador, but this crevice of a room didn't allow for it; it was the closest he'd been to one of them and could even see the dull, straight line of her teeth when she spoke.

Her snout was small and rounded, her mane brown. The strands were incredibly fine, too many to count, and it was pulled atop her head to reveal pale, pinkish skin, broken only by dark specks across her cheeks. Blue spindling veins at her wrists and larger ones along the sides of her neck pulsed rapidly with her heart, while her eyes—typical to her kind—were white, with a circle of blue. His ear twitched. Humans' small, half-colorless orbs were decidedly unappealing.

Loose white material covered her legs and torso, and left most of her bone-thin arms bare; it was the exact opposite of what he knew female to be. Askari females were sometimes larger than males, tended to match them in strength, and were more aggressive. He had thought the males of her race fragile and weak-looking, but she was even more so—the first human female he'd come into contact with and he had to wonder how her species had survived. How could such a creature bear young, protect them, teach them to protect themselves, all without breaking? He couldn't even imagine her surviving the breeding act itself, she was so sickeningly small and withered looking.

Aderus shifted uncomfortably as she stepped closer.

A soft, monotone voice drew his attention. "Okay, I'm going to try and make this as painless as possible, but it still may hurt a little," she said, looking at his arm. She hesitated, meeting his gaze. She appeared to be waiting for something...

"You may proceed." He rumbled, granting her permission.

"Okay," she breathed, shoulders relaxing, and cautiously stepped forward to lightly grip his arm. "I got the impression you don't really like to be touched..." Her eyes flicked up again, questioning perhaps. "I didn't mean to offend."

She was referring to her advancing on him before but the fact he had accepted her hand offer earlier gave him pause. Aderus chalked it up to impulse, or curiosity, or the fact she was absurdly non-threatening. But then, wasn't that what their situation now required? Obliging behavior? Diplomacy? Obliging was not a word used to describe his race.

White gloves covered her short, blunt fingers as they rested lightly against his arm. His nostrils twitched. Her scent was stronger, more discernible now that she was so close without others around. Alien. But not repulsive.

There were only a few races with which his kind willingly interacted and fewer still that appeared so similar in form. Their more detached nature, combined with an inherent ferocity and such predatory characteristics, tended to deter most other life forms, so it wasn't often that they interacted this closely. He watched her carefully as she worked, attuned to her movements. They seemed to be very telling of her emotions and Aderus tried hard to put them together—match expressions and scents to emotions as best he could.

"It is an invasion of privacy," he responded after a time, still watching her carefully.

She paused with her head bent over his arm. "Oh. You mean like personal space?"

It took him a moment to grasp the meaning of her words. "It gives one an unfair advantage," he countered as his gaze fixed on her hand. "Your fingers tremor and your heart has increased. Although you appear calm, you are not."

At that, the small female grew impossibly still. Without lifting her head, she replied, "you can *feel* my heartbeat?"

"And hear it. But when you are touching me, as you are now, that sense overpowers the other."

***

Tori froze at the large Demon's revelation, then lifted her hands from him and took a step back. *Okay, that creeped her out.*

"I'm sorry," she said with a nervous chuckle, as she struggled to regain her composure. "I just...that's a tad unsettling. Humans don't have those abilities."

She looked up to find him watching her, his face expressionless. "From what I have observed, our senses are much more evolved." He paused. "Now you understand why we avoid touching."

She did understand. It was harder to hide how you were feeling. Which gave way to a single panicked thought.

"You can't...sense...a person's *thoughts,* can you?" She felt a little ridiculous asking, but that didn't stop the sinking feeling in her chest at the possibility.

What appeared to be secondary eyelids slid across his eyes in a blink. "No."

Phew.

Relieved, she cleared her throat and stepped forward again, determined to finish treating his arm.

"I'll be honest then, you are intimidating," she said slowly as she worked, her gaze flicking to meet his. "But, I know it's just a matter of getting used to our differences," she added, as much for herself as for him as she tried her best to move past the *alien in the room* to focus on the task at hand. Tori lowered her head to study the wound again, aware of how she was eye level with his torso.

Her brow furrowed. Odd. Was she seeing things or did the gashes seem shallower? They also no longer oozed blood as they had just minutes before. She specifically remembered because she'd noted with interest that it was much darker than human blood, a red-black almost. The edges actually looked healed, but that was impossible!

"What is... These..." she murmured, running her gloved fingers lightly over said edges.

"They are healing," he rumbled above her, and she startled, disconcerted with how easily he seemed to read her.

"That's—" Tori floundered. "So then, these will be completely gone soon?"

He was silent, gaze almost calculating. "Yes."

From a medical standpoint, it was beyond amazing. There *were* drugs that worked to accelerate healing in people, but nothing that compared to his kind's innate ability. Researchers pushed, but the results always led to some form of cancer or autoimmune disorder and they still hadn't figured out a way to eliminate scarring. She suddenly felt inadequate as a species, and her confusion only grew.

"I don't understand. I mean, do you just need me to disinfect the wound? Maybe I can help with some of the more severe injuries?" she added, her mind quickly churning. Why accept her offer if he'd be healed soon? A ribbon of fear wound its way up her spine, but she pushed it down. *There are armed guards not twenty feet away. It's perfectly safe.*

But as he pinned her with a cold, rapacious stare, she wasn't sure of anything. Never had someone stared at her like that, and Tori couldn't say she liked it. She fidgeted, wondering what was going through his head. They seemed very reluctant to accept any hands-on medical help so far.

His intense gaze flicked behind her, almost anxiously...

Something else was going on here. Was he perhaps trying to tell her something, ask for help? She tried to follow his train of thought.

"Just a precaution...and they're standing far enough away, they can't hear us," she blurted, thinking to ease him. "We have strict laws concerning privacy, especially when it comes to medical information."

He looked back at her and his gold and black eyes narrowed ever so slightly. Or maybe it was just his irises? Fascinating. Was he was trying to decide if he could trust her with something? Tori desperately wanted to pass that test. What seemed like forever passed before he finally spoke.

"You want to help us." It was a statement.

"Yes, I do," she said softly, waiting for him to continue.

"Please excuse the interruption," a voice boomed behind her.

Tori started and turned to see Wells hovering just outside the exam room. He looked to Aderus, who immediately stood from the table.

"Err...Representative Jadar was looking for you," Wells explained, stepping aside. A body filled the doorway and who she assumed was Jadar ducked to enter the small exam room. Where Aderus's hair was dark, this one's was almost mahogany, but he had the same graphite-colored skin. He straightened and looked right at her patient, which was when Tori noticed his eyes—a vivid, glittering green. She tried not to stare, but just as with Aderus, it was hard to look away. She did have to admit being more partial to gold than green and the space suddenly felt cramped as she stood between two big bodies.

Tori's gaze moved between them, waiting for either to speak, until she realized those green eyes were fixed on her, as if he just noticed she was there. He blinked twice, and his nostrils flared. Feeling awkward, she gave a small smile.

"Hello, I'm Tori," she said, looking up at him, this time catching herself from extending a hand. "I'm assuming you're Jadar? It's nice to meet you."

The male didn't say anything, just stared her up and down and looked back at Aderus. It was like they were silently communicating.

Aderus finally spoke. "He is most like our equivalent of what you do."

"Oh," she responded, looking to Jadar with raised brows. "In that case, it really is nice to meet you. Anything I can do to help, please, let me know." She gushed, more than eager to assist an alien counterpart.

"Thank you," he finally responded. His voice was a little softer, but still carried that two-toned quality.

They both began another wordless exchange and Tori got the hint. With a tight smile, she went to stand out in the hallway with Wells and the guards.

Chapter Four

"I thought we were not accepting help from their *doctors*."

Jadar stood blocking the entrance to the exam room. He was tense, anxious, apparent by the backward stoop of his ears and curled claws.

"How are the others?" Aderus countered.

Jadar's mood did not lighten. "The one called Braxas is still unconscious. Did you know there is a *palkriv* on board?"

Aderus blinked.

He thought back to the brief gathering they'd had in the ship's hold before docking with the Earth vessel. He definitely would have noticed a *palkriv,* but that was also the reason one wouldn't have been there among the rest.

"He lives?"

The *khurzhev's* expression remained unchanged. "For now."

Aderus was silent as he thought on this newfound dilemma. It was rare to see a full-grown *palkriv*. Most did not survive into adulthood and that just attested to this one's strength and ferocity. He doubted the male would allow any of them near him while conscious.

Jadar's stance shifted, but his attention never left Aderus. "Does she belong to a different species? She appears unnaturally small." Aderus knew he was referring to Tori.

"I do not know. She is the only one I've seen."

"She does not seem strong enough to birth a brood, much less protect one. One of our younglings would outweigh her two-fold."

Aderus looked up with a pointed stare. "I do not understand it either, but she has been less fearful than most of their soldiers."

The green-eyed male's snout twitched once with guarded interest. Aderus was just as wary. He did not know what human deception looked like but was sure of its presence. Their situation demanded a decision, however, and the others had volunteered him to negotiate.

They had to trust one of them.

***

As soon as Tori exited the exam room, the ambassador approached with the practiced smile of a politician. "Dr. Davis, if I may."

She felt a light but insistent touch on her elbow, steering her off to the side before she could even respond. Wells stood blocking her view to the exam room and the smile instantly dropped from his lips. "Listen closely." His voice turned low and commanding. "You are the only one they've allowed near them so far. I know you're a very intelligent individual, so you understand the unique and invaluable position that puts you in. It is imperative you gather as much information as possible, anything and everything you can learn about them, and report back to me." Tori blinked, taken aback.

"I'm not a spy, Ambassador," she said slowly, not quite believing what she was hearing and still reeling from his abrupt change in demeanor.

"Right now, you are what we need you to be." His brown eyes were hard and serious. "Our planet's entire existence could very well be at stake. We have no way of knowing what their actual intentions are, and most importantly, what they're capable of. So, I'll say it again—anything and everything."

Tori wet her lips, unused to being spoken to—no, not spoken, *dictated* to in such a manner. "I-I'll be sure to inform you right away if I see or hear anything threatening."

A muscle twitched in the man's jaw. "I'm not certain we're understanding each other, Doctor."

Tori felt her hackles rise. She knew what the diplomat wanted, but she didn't agree. Trust was paramount in any relationship; as a doctor she understood that better than most. But first contact with an intelligent alien race? Multiply that by a thousand. By some miracle, she had gotten Aderus to trust her enough not only to let her treat him, but she was sure he'd been about to reveal something extremely important in that exam room and she wasn't about to jeopardize the progress she'd made to play double-o-seven for Team Earth. It wasn't that she didn't understand the gravity of the situation either. The ambassador was right. Their position *was very* real and *very* dangerous. All the more reason not to do anything stupid. Their "guests" possessed highly developed senses, were freakishly perceptive, and she was no trained operative. She'd probably give herself away in less than a minute. Plus, she wasn't military—he couldn't just order her about!

"Oh no," she said in a falsely sweet voice. "I understand completely, sir. If you'll excuse me."

Tori stepped around him and headed back toward the exam room. She stopped just outside, took a calming breath, and looked to where the mahogany-haired Demon and Aderus were talking. But what they were speaking wasn't English. The language seemed to utilize their unusual vocal cords—hard consonants and hisses set above guttural rumbling and growls. It was fascinating to listen to, and she found herself straining to hear...until she caught the ambassador approaching again from the corner of her eye.

Shit. It seemed their conversation wasn't over.

"You may finish treating my arm." Tori whipped about at the sound of Aderus's distinctive voice. He was standing just outside the exam room, blocking the doorway completely with his tall frame. His sharp gaze moved briefly between her and Wells, and the diplomat's mood lightened instantly. "Of course," he said, gesturing to her.

Tori approached her patient, eager to get away from the man and his demands. Politics. She knew the game, understood how it was played, maybe even the necessity of it at times, but that didn't mean she had to like it or the people involved. Her job was helping people, healing them, plain and simple. Now they were sitting her down and trying to force her to play. *Not fucking likely*. She'd do exactly as she told him; be alert, observant, and of course if she discovered anything menacing, she'd report back right away. But something in her gut made her want to believe that Aderus and his kind weren't a threat to them. Unless, of course, the higher-ups did something stupid...like provoke them.

Tori stopped a foot from the large Demon and tipped her head back. She noticed his hand covered his arm, hiding the wounds. "Shall we go back inside the exam room?"

He shot a calculating look to Wells one last time, then turned and ducked into the tiny room. She followed and was surprised to find Jadar still there. He stood in the corner, watching. "Oh, hello again. I thought you'd left, but you're certainly welcome to stay, if you like. I-I mean, not that you need my permission," she fumbled, feeling her cheeks heat. She had no idea what was customary for them.

He angled his head and she heard an odd sound.

Tori blinked and looked back to Aderus, but his expression remained blank.

Ohh-kay.

At first glance, their race came across as alarmingly predatory, mostly due to their appearance. But she also observed that they were incredibly stoic, near impossible to read. Their faces were expressionless, their reactions extremely tempered, so that if you blinked, you missed it...which is why she found herself *thinking* she saw something, because in the next instant, it was gone. Humans probably seemed overly expressive in comparison, she thought, which might partly explain their keen perception. Well, that, and some very highly developed senses. Kind of hard to fool someone when they could *smell* your fear and *hear* your heart pounding.

Aderus uncovered his arm and Tori stepped closer. She leaned forward but took care not to touch him, then shook her head in amazement.

"If you were human, I'd say those look days old. That's incredible."

When she looked up, it was to find Aderus watching her again. Their stares were unnerving. Especially with such otherworldly eyes.

"I think we're done here," she breathed, straightening and taking a step back. "But, my offer still stands," she said, snapping off her gloves. "If you need and are comfortable with my helping with anything else, just let me know. Supplies...anything." She stood waiting patiently, hopeful. This was his chance to finish what he had been trying to tell her before. Tori tried not to fidget.

His gaze never left her, and it took him what seemed like forever to respond.

"You must come aboard our ship."

Chapter Five

Tori tried to remain calm as they moved through the various airlocks connecting the *Amendment* to its guest ship. Her legs felt weak and shaky, her heart thumped along. *The stress of this day alone is probably enough to take a full year off my life*, she thought irritably, not used to feeling so on edge. Then again, she was always the one in control and so far, the last few hours had been...shockingly surreal to say the least, a real test of her mental fortitude.

She didn't know what she'd been expecting to hear from the large alien ahead of her in that exam room, but it certainly hadn't involved this. She was far from comfortable being the only person allowed to board their ship but chose to trust Aderus and his words that no harm would come to her.

It's not like Wells had really fought very hard otherwise. The zealous look in the diplomat's light brown eyes had almost made her sick. She knew he saw it as the ideal opportunity to gain information.

Tori felt a surge of anger. Well, let him think that, because she wasn't giving him shit. How fucked up was it when you had to trust assurances from an extraterrestrial you'd only known a couple of hours over your own species, because they obviously didn't give a damn? So what if something happened to her. Sacrifices have to be made, right?

Wells *had* tried to insist Tori be accompanied by two military guards, but she knew it wasn't out of concern for her personal safety when he'd given in easily enough at the two Demon's firm refusals. She took a calming breath and instead tried to keep her mind on the task at hand.

They weren't telling her much. Just that there was someone badly injured and they wanted her help assessing the situation, seeing what supplies could be provided, et cetera.

Tori couldn't deny a certain sense of pride she felt at making that connection. At being the only human being they trusted so far to let come aboard their ship. She chose to focus on that feeling.

The hair along the back of her neck stiffened, and she suppressed the urge to look back. The Demon that trailed her was a few inches shorter than Aderus, still over a head taller than her, and had long silvery braids—it's what she had chosen to call their hair because that's what the thick, textured locks reminded her of. His complexion was a shade lighter than Jadar and Aderus, though still dark, and his eyes were...freakish. Sky blue with streaks of white that radiated out from the center like spokes on an old wagon wheel she'd once seen in a history vid.

His odd coloring had caused her to stare a little longer than necessary when they'd met, and his strange eyes had been fixated on her ever since.

The three of them moved into the Decon chamber and two heavy metal doors sealed off the room. Tori widened her stance, legs in line with her hips, and raised her arms out to the sides. She did it without thought, having gone through the procedure countless times prepping for surgery or moving between vessels. She closed her eyes to the brief, but powerful bursts of air laced with sterilizers.

The hiss and pop of the sealed door in front of them opening had her noting that her escorts hadn't moved from their rigid stances. Aderus started forward into the next chamber, which connected directly with the Demon ship.

Tori followed slowly. There was a short corridor and the door behind them, the one leading back to the *Amendment*, sealed and locked. A chill ran down her spine. *No turning back.* She was completely at their mercy now and sincerely hoped that trusting them hadn't been a mistake.

As they approached the last airlock, the one connected to their vessel, Tori stopped, marveling at the unique metal-looking material. It reminded her of the same black fabric that composed their uniforms, only she watched as a glimmer of light seemed to move across it, like a wave. She blinked, fascinated.

The doors parted and Aderus advanced, no longer needing to duck. Tori hesitated, peering into the antechamber at her first glimpse of an alien vessel, at an object not from Earth. That realization made the already intense experience even more profound.

It seemed the entire ship was made of the strange black metal, and the glimmering waves of blue-green light that flowed through it illuminated the floor and walls. It was a soft glow, nothing like the harsh, grating lights of the *Amendment*. As her eyes adjusted, she could make out only smooth flowing lines and curves, no hard angles or edges.

An odd tingle at the back of her neck distracted her and Tori instinctually turned. She jerked hard on a gasp as the Demon with the eerie eyes—Krim, as he called himself—leaned over her. At her startled reaction, he quickly pulled back.

"Good Reason, you nearly gave me a heart attack!" she exclaimed and adjusted the shoulder strap of the small supplies tote she carried across her chest. "Please don't do that." She watched warily as he relaxed his stance. She didn't know what he'd been doing, but it made her *really* uncomfortable.

Deep, loud clicking made her whip her head around. Aderus stood not three feet away, his gaze locked on Krim, and it took a moment to realize the sound was coming from him. It ascended in pitch and sent chills down Tori's spine, reminding her of something from a horror vid. The other Demon blinked and took a step back. *A warning then...*

Aderus's golden gaze locked on Krim a moment longer before he moved aside. Tori swallowed. It was quickly becoming evident they were more reliant on sounds to communicate than actual language. She moved forward slowly, feeling their eyes on her.

The sound of doors sealing shut locked the three of them in a small room, and Tori started when she felt the oddest sensation begin in her feet; a mild tingling that quickly intensified, causing her heart to skip. It felt like her skin was *crawling*, as if she could feel thousands of little legs inching across her flesh. She looked down, half expecting that to be the case, but there was nothing.

What the hell is happening? she thought, her gaze quickly finding her escorts. Were they experiencing it, too, or were these tricks of her overstimulated brain right now? Aderus hadn't mentioned to expect anything, so...

In fact, he and Krim were just standing there, as if waiting for something, and to Tori's horror the sensation began moving up her legs. The feeling would have made anyone uneasy, but creepy crawlies really freaked her out. Bats, rats, snakes? Totally fine. Bugs? They were one of the things gladly left back on Earth. And that's exactly what this felt like.

Her eyes went wide as it continued, she broke into a cold sweat, and the thin tether she had on her self-control snapped. Her hand flew out and latched onto Aderus' forearm. It was like a replay of earlier, only a little less intense. The flesh beneath her hand was hard and he turned on her, upper lip twitching. Tori released him, realizing what she'd done, but he must have seen her look of terror.

"Something's wrong. It feels like—my skin is crawling!" She heard how pinched her voice sounded as the nightmarish sensation progressed up her legs. Something akin to understanding flashed across his strong, alien features.

"Remain still."

Right, Tori thought to herself, *just stand still while that lurid crawling moves up my thighs, my groin, my waist...chest, neck, face.*

***

"She is distressed."

Aderus had been watching the small female the entire time from the corner of his eye; he knew what Krim said was true. Her heart was pounding so loudly he could almost feel it, had felt it when she'd touched him.

They did not react as these humans did. To show fear was to show weakness, and nothing triggered their baser instincts more. He didn't understand why she was acting the way she was, but they had to go through decontamination to enter the ship.

He was about to demand she calm when the Earther latched on to his arm with a grip that surprised him. He hissed and tensed, barely suppressing the urge to attack. It was obvious her kind thought nothing of grabbing at each other, but to him, such an act was highly offensive and usually preceded a vicious exchange of blows.

"I'm sorry, I really am. I just...need something else to focus on."

The *doctor* looked up then, eyes wide, her face void of color. Her voice sounded strange. What she said made no sense, but Aderus needed her aboard their vessel, so he leashed his impulses. He wanted her hand off of him. Even during the most intimate of acts—breeding—Askari did not engage in any unnecessary contact. The "touching" that *was* exchanged likely considered by her race to be violent, almost brutal.

She released him with a shaky breath as soon as the process was over.

"Thank you," she breathed, her flesh an odd red hue. "I hope I didn't make you too uncomfortable." She paused. "Physical contact sometimes helps when we're panicked or fearful."

Chapter Six

Tori was relieved as they left the alien vessel's Decon chamber. She'd been on the edge of an honest-to-Gaia panic attack and it had been embarrassing. *Way to represent my species, my profession, and my gender*, she derided herself. At the time, her thought had just been to get through it and it had been all she could think of to grab Aderus's arm for strength. She just hoped she hadn't made him too uncomfortable. He hadn't said anything in response to her apology and explanation.

She risked a glance back at Krim. His head was angled, and Tori blinked when one corner of his mouth rose briefly in an almost half-smile before she quickly faced forward again. Did they actually smile? She pictured what that would look like with their double sets of sharp silvery teeth. *Fucking creepy.*

Aderus led them through a series of hallways, pulses of light from the black metal setting a soothing, zen-like tone. The walls widened as they approached a large intersection and she glanced to the right. It opened into a space littered with debris and sporadic blue flames. Tori couldn't help but be curious about the technology that had enabled them to traverse galaxies. Just the thought was mind-blowing. But as she stood staring, movement caught her eye. The room wasn't empty. He must have been down behind the large, twisted pieces of metal before, but now stood facing her. Fiery orange eyes. This one wore his dark braids back, drawing attention to his long, pointed ears.

It was only a glimpse before a massive torso blocked her view. Aderus stood close enough, Tori could feel the heat radiating from his body. It was something she'd noticed when she examined him; his kind ran hot. She guessed a good ten degrees hotter than a human. She took pleasure in the fleeting warmth (their ship was a lot cooler than what she considered comfortable) before looking up into blazing eyes.

Her stomach dropped.

"This way," he rumbled, and it occurred to her how her behavior must look.

No doubt Aderus had an idea the governments desired access to their technology, they weren't stupid. And she'd just made herself appear as the exact thing she refused she'd be.

Tori dropped her gaze. "I'm sorry, I didn't mean to gawk. If you'll lead the way, I'll to keep my eyes to myself."

She followed at a respectable distance, trying to keep pace with the large alien's strides. They meandered through the ship, passing numerous corridors and rooms, none of which she gave more than a passing glance. She'd raised enough suspicion from her earlier fly-catching episode. The ship was much bigger than it seemed from the outside. Tori tried to ignore the attention she drew from the few Demon they did encounter, their penetrating stares as she passed making her fidgety. She felt like a specimen on display. It made her wonder how they perceived her, how they perceived humans. Quick glances confirmed most had the same deep graphite-colored skin as Aderus—some darker, bordering on true black, some lighter, like Krim. Her restlessness and unfamiliarity with the ship made minutes seem like hours until finally they came upon a room in a curved corridor. It was empty, save a long, high table to the right and reminded her of an exam room. She voiced the observation aloud.

"Yes," Aderus answered in that deep dual tone as he moved to the far wall. He wasn't looking at her but was focused on the wall, his hand moving over some invisible panel that suddenly lit with a green glow. It then projected from the wall, and his long fingers moved fluidly, interacting with displays that were suspended in midair. Tori stood watching him, transfixed. Interactive holographic technology (IHoT for short) was still in its early stages on Earth. Not as mind-boggling as space warping, but impressive nonetheless.

She recovered from her fascination and began observing his profile. They were intimidating up close. His black and gold stare unnerved her, like he was taking in every detail. You felt vulnerable, exposed. But he wasn't leveling that gaze on her now, so her eyes could travel freely over his form. Their uniforms made it difficult to make out details unless you really looked, which she hadn't had the opportunity to do until now. Toned flesh, lithe and graceful. His limbs were longer than a human's, the joints in slightly different places. Something about his legs seemed unusual, too—he held himself differently—and Tori realized it was his feet. She couldn't make out much with the coverings they wore though. Not shoes, per se. It looked like an extension of the uniform. Her gaze moved up, to his pointed ears and strange sleek locks. *What would they feel like?* she wondered.

Her eyes widened. What was she doing?

A certain degree of interest would be natural, considering their humanoid-like appearance, she told herself. But this was not the time or place to indulge in aberrant xenophilic fantasies.

Head in the game, Davis!

Tori felt her cheeks heat before she steeled herself. Aderus finished what he was doing, stepping away from the panel, and the wall they were facing suddenly morphed into a large view screen; a welcome distraction.

Tori was taken aback at what she saw. A pale Demon sat hunched over on the floor in the corner of a room. She had thought they were all dark-skinned. People said she was white, but next to him her pallor definitely had a fleshy hue. Concern grew as she took in his ravaged state. His head was lowered, arms at his sides, long locks matted with what she assumed was dried blood. It hung forward, hiding his face. Deep gashes covered his back and arms, his uniform—Oh Gaia, his flesh—hanging in pieces off his body. The poor thing looked like he'd been brutalized.

"Good Gods, what happened to him?" Tori exclaimed, looking to Aderus.

The wounds were deep and gaping. She was amazed how he even managed to hold himself upright. A human man in his condition would most likely be unconscious, and it reminded her again of exactly who and what she was dealing with.

Aderus's eyes locked with hers. "He will die. Soon, if he cannot heal."

"I can see that," she responded, itching to take action. What the hell were they standing around for? "Is there a reason you haven't treated him?"

"Yes."

Tori waited for him to elaborate, but he remained silent. She was confused and growing more inpatient by the second. The individual on the other side of that view screen needed help. Now!

"If you'll allow me, I'll see to his wounds."

Aderus watched her. "You said you wanted to help," he rumbled, repeating her words from earlier.

"Yes, of course. Whatever you need," she responded anxiously.

"Blood."

Tori's brows shot up. "I'm sorry, what?" She glanced back at Krim, suddenly more than a little uneasy. He stood watching her as well, his pale blue-and-white-streaked eyes unmoving.

"I-I don't understand."

"We supplement from other Askari when wounds are severe." His eyes moved down her body. "Our species are more similar than different." He paused, almost hesitant. "There are others. Too many for us to help."

Right. *Was he crazy?* He wanted to transfuse them with *human* blood?

"What—*how* could that even be possible?" she heard herself say slowly. "We can't even take blood from other humans unless they're the same blood type. There's no way a transfusion would be biologically or chemically—"

"We consume blood."

Tori's stomach dropped. Those three little words, and she was suddenly very close to that wall in her mind, the one that set the limit on how much reality-altering shit she could process in one day. It felt like the plotline for some twisted sci-fi movie, the whole day had, and she had to remind herself this was reality.

"I—" Tori broke off to swallow and lick her lips. "I need to sit down." Combined with her plummeting blood sugar, she needed a seat before she made friends with the floor. She moved on weak legs to the table, which she vaguely noted seemed to be hovering in midair, no legs. It was level with her chest, so she leaned over it. "I'm sorry, but would one of you please help me onto this thing?"

Talk about embarrassing. It was silent, neither one of them moving to help her. They were probably unsure how to respond.

Then she heard a short, throaty hiss. Tori sucked in a breath when a thick, dark arm wrapped around her from behind and lifted her off the floor. She leaned forward to balance her weight, gripping the forearm with both hands and her eyes went wide when a large hand palmed her ass to turn and set her on the table.

Aderus stepped back, golden eyes flashing, and she could feel the heat creep into her cheeks, which, considering she was probably pasty pale, made her look almost normal. "Ah, thank you." Her skin tingled, but she ignored it and reached trembling fingers down into her supplies tote, relieved to find what she was looking for. Tori held the glucose jet injector pen to the side of her neck and pressed the button. There was a slight pinch, but within seconds most of the trembling stopped and she felt better.

Aderus eyed her, his chin tipping as if scenting the air. "Are you ill?"

"No. I'm fine, thank you," she lied. "I just got a bit shaky because I haven't eaten today, and it's been a lot to process. I'm feeling better now." Tori took a deep, steadying breath. "How...how exactly is it you think that we can help you?" she said slowly.

"Humans get sick if they don't eat frequently?" he asked, ignoring her question.

"Sometimes," she answered. "But I'm fine now."

He studied her a moment longer. Was it her imagination, or were his ears standing more erect?

"Our species evolved in similar atmospheres with parallel biology. Earth's metals and minerals are like those of our home world, so the nutrients we need are present."

Aderus stared at her, straight-faced.

Christ, he's serious.

An uneasy tremor wracked her body. "Wouldn't...*consuming* it make you ill, though? I mean, regardless of if our blood is..." *Ugh*. "...digestible for you, there are microbes, viruses—"

"The decontamination process eliminates anything harmful. We do not digest it as you are thinking."

Was he saying that some weird laser in the chamber had penetrated her skin to essentially "neutralize" her blood? Had *that* been the gross crawling sensation? It was more than enough to wrap her head around. She didn't even bother to question his last comment. Instead she nodded numbly, because what else was she to do?

Tori's gaze moved to the pale Demon on the view screen, his flesh literally hanging from his bones. If she could in any way help to ease that poor creature's suffering, was there really a choice? This was what she did, it was who she was.

"How much do you need?" she asked, trying to keep her voice steady.

Chapter Seven

"What are you doing?" he asked, as she attached the small needleless catheter to the skin just above the vein in her left arm. Krim stepped closer, watching as well. It occurred to her they might have had other ideas, but she just as quickly decided she was uncomfortable enough with the situation, and the supplies had been in her tote.

"Helping him," she finally answered, focused on her arm.

She felt her heart skip as Aderus moved closer. Her legs dangled off the table, arm outstretched, as bright red liquid ran from her arm into the bag. Tori couldn't quite believe she was doing this as she clenched and unclenched her fist to pump the blood faster. She heard a sniff.

I feel like food, she thought, tensing.

Her gaze flicked back to the view screen. He was shaking now, violent tremors racking the torn and battered flesh of his back and upper arms as he struggled to keep himself upright.

Tori quickly sealed and detached the bag a few moments later, holding it out.

"Is that enough?"

Aderus reached out to take it from her, turning it slowly in his long-fingered hand. Krim's gaze was on the pint as well.

He tilted his head, eyes traveling over her slumped form.

"You are not well."

I've been better. "I'll be fine. Give him the pint," she said wearily, nodding to the male on the view screen.

***

Aderus exchanged a look with Krim. He could still smell the curious tang of her blood in the air as he turned the warm pouch over in his hand. It was likely enough to save the *palkriv*. But he could not, in good conscience, let even a *palkriv* consume untested blood. So, he carefully punctured a small hole in the soft material with the tip of one claw.

He sniffed cautiously. Scans of her physiology had revealed its most notable difference—a peculiarity involving the molecule used to transport oxygen. It was highly uncommon to feed from other species and he seldom heard the experience described as pleasant, but the Earther's blood didn't scent too aversely. He forced his tongue out in a quick swipe over his claw.

The initial sweetness made him cringe, but the metallic aftertaste was surprisingly palatable. The barest hint of a heavy, warm feeling washed over him, and he tensed in alarm. But it passed quickly, making him wonder if perhaps he'd imagined it.

"What is it?" Krim rumbled at him in their own language. Aderus curled his lip at the sharp-eyed male in annoyance.

"It is...different," he finally supplied, as if that were all the explanation necessary. But not harmful, as far as he could tell. And the sooner he got the offering to the *palkriv*, the sooner she could get back to her ship. He didn't know much about humans, but she did not look well.

***

Tori watched Aderus leave with the pint. She lifted her head expectantly and straightened when she saw him appear on the view screen moments later.

He stood in the doorway, the bloodied male trembling weakly on the floor in the corner. Aderus rumbled something and instantly the male's whole demeanor changed. He stiffened, his body going rigid, as he jerked into a crouch and hissed deeply at Aderus. Tori's eyes widened as she got her first good look at his face. His eyes were crimson. And his lips were frighteningly drawn back revealing double sets of sharp teeth. She stifled a gasp as he lunged violently at Aderus only to be stopped mere inches from contact by some invisible barrier. He backed off a fraction but stood facing him nose to nose, only the barrier separating them. The glare he leveled sent chills up her spine. If looks could kill. She knew if the barrier wasn't there that's exactly what this male would try to do. But Tori didn't understand his reaction. Aderus was trying to help him. And how was he even physically able? He looked on death's door only seconds before. As Tori watched, however, she caught the tremor in his frame, which only seemed to worsen as the seconds ticked by.

"Why is he not giving it to him?" she asked Krim, confused and growing agitated.

The other Demon watched her, and Tori reflexively gripped the metal table under her hands as she stared back.

"It is his decision to accept."

She realized two things right then: One, the extraterrestrials before her were an infuriatingly stubborn and untamed race (or maybe it was just the men, which made her wonder about their women) and two, the injured one on the view screen, whom she went to all that trouble to help, looked like he'd sooner die staring down his opponent than accept aid.

Tori let out a frustrated breath. This was ridiculous. "Okay then," she muttered, sliding carefully off the table, steadying herself with one hand. She saw from the corner of her eye Krim's relaxed stance change instantly.

"Could you please take me to them? Perhaps I can change his mind."

He glanced quickly down her body. "You are weak."

Actually, Tori was mentally, physically, and emotionally drained. She'd just willingly donated a pint of her own blood to help an alien she didn't know, which consequently had her feeling much shittier, and of course, he wasn't accepting it. Now, she had a creature that looked like he could bench press a car making her feel even more pathetic, and that kind of irritated her. Just a little bit. Next to them, she *was* weak, and she was getting the sense that was something they didn't respect. But she wasn't a damn invalid! She was a human doctor trying to provide aid to a race of super-beings. *Super-predators,* she thought more aptly.

Her mind warned that it was the blood loss and lack of food talking, but Tori's eyes flashed as she turned to face him fully, letting go of the table. She clenched her fists at her sides and drew herself up.

"I appreciate the concern, but I'm fine," she said firmly. "I'm asking you to please take me to them. I can't sit here and watch him deteriorate unnecessarily. He might think differently if I talk to him."

Krim's chilling, streaked eyes suddenly changed. It felt…menacing, which gave her pause, but Tori refused to back down. Even when he stepped closer and lifted his chin, all the while keeping his gaze locked with hers. It hit her that her behavior might be provoking something, or initiating it. The blue-eyed Askari had been pretty mellow, if not overly curious, up until now, but he suddenly seemed very engaged. It freaked her out because she had no idea how to handle him, no idea what this change in behavior might mean. There was also the little fact she was alone in this room with the one who swore her safety nowhere in sight.

She couldn't say whether it was pride, or instinct that whispered in her ear, telling her to stare him down and not move a muscle, but Tori did both, and eventually he backed off. Some of the tension drained away and she let herself relax, taking a breath.

He was silent, nose wrinkling. Something she couldn't place flashed across his features.

"I will take you."

***

Tori trailed behind Krim right up until they reached Aderus, who had stepped away from the barrier as soon as he spotted Krim. His golden gaze immediately found her then flashed back up to her escort.

He didn't seem pleased. She wasn't surprised.

If he had been okay with her being there, he would have invited her along in the first place. What she didn't expect was how he moved to stand in front of her, forcing her to the side. She backed up against the wall to avoid bumping him. He faced Krim, speaking in clipped rumbles and hisses. Her eyes traveled up his back to the dark points of his ears rising prominently above his head. She slapped herself out of it and stepped around him, breaking into their conversation.

"I can tell you're not pleased," she said, looking up to Aderus, who instantly quieted and looked down at her. It probably wasn't polite to interrupt their conversation, but Tori would worry over propriety later; for now, she didn't think they had time. "I demanded Krim take me to you, and I'm sorry if I'm overstepping my bounds, but I can't just stand by while that man dies because his pride won't let him accept help or something equally stupid. If there's even a small chance I can convince him then that's why I'm here."

Tori paused to take a breath, half expecting Aderus to shut her down, but instead, that same look flashed in his eyes, as with Krim back in the exam room. She held his gaze and pushed on, even as her heart pounded in her chest.

"I'm here to help, Aderus. Please. Let me do that," she tried, softening her tone. She hesitated only slightly then held her hand out for the pint, keeping her eyes locked on his.

He watched her for long moments, something she was growing used to. His gaze would occasionally flick down her body and back up, but she was getting much better at holding it without looking away. And it was in that moment, a light went on and Tori realized what he was doing; he was reading her body language. She remembered being told their primary means of communication was non-verbal, but she'd not fully understood it until now. It shed light on Aderus and Jadar's interactions before, and the exam room just now, she thought, her eyes widening in comprehension. She needed to be much more aware of her body language.

Something dropped into her hand, pulling her from her thoughts. The pint. She looked up to Aderus, his expression unreadable again.

She flashed him a smile, relieved and grateful he was willing to give her a chance. "Thank you," she said, then turned quickly, not wanting them to change their minds. Tori took a steadying breath and rolled her shoulders, determined to talk down the injured male.

He must have heard her voice, because when she inched into view he was standing to the side, glancing down the corridor so that his crimson eyes were the first thing she saw. Large, ringed with black, and set against milky-white skin, his coloring made him the most striking of his kind she'd seen so far. Then she looked down at his gaping wounds and clenched her teeth.

"Hi there," she said gently. "My name is Tori."

The male's stance was rigid, battle-ready, but when he saw her he jerked and blinked. Frozen in place, his eyes traveled over her as if in awe. She knew she was likely the first human he'd met. Then Tori noticed how he stared repeatedly at her exposed skin—her arms, neck, and finally her face. His eyes flicked back down to her bare arms.

Tori frowned. Just how rare was light skin for them??

"I know, you and I could be distantly related," she joked, trying to put him at ease. It was obvious he didn't trust Aderus or Krim. "Us pale people gotta stick together, right?"

At that, he jerked his gaze up to hers and held it. *Bingo*.

"Do you have a name?" Silence. More staring. At least he wasn't trying to attack her through the barrier like he'd done with Aderus and he wasn't flashing those vicious-looking teeth.

"I was hoping you'd let me help you," she continued, holding up the pint. "I really want to help you." He glanced quickly to the bag then back again, his breathing growing shallower and the trembling worse. He was deteriorating fast.

"I'm a doctor, and it's what I do: heal people, in whatever way I can. Apparently, we're compatible donors for your species." She paused. To hear herself say it aloud sounded crazy, but she didn't have time to dwell on that right now.

"Please. Take it." Tori held her breath as she waited for some type of response from him.

She thought she saw a pained look cross his face a moment before he stepped back, away from the barrier. The trembling was severe now and on the second step back he stumbled, swaying for a moment before righting himself. The bright red eyes that had stayed fixed on her began to flutter and Tori didn't think he was going to last much longer.

"You need to sit. Right now," she said sternly, not wanting a fall to cause more unnecessary damage. As if on cue, his legs gave way, dropping him to the floor, where he sat propped against the wall. His head drooped, but his eyes stayed on her, as if he didn't want to break the connection. Tori could hear shallow, labored breathing and her instincts kicked in, urging her to act. She looked back for Aderus and started at finding him right next to her, the wall to her right blocking him from view.

"He just collapsed but backed away. Can we go in with the bag?" she asked hurriedly, looking up at him. In her experience, the situation would have been critical and though she knew they were physically far superior, like comparing an old gasoline-powered car to a fusion-fed jet, she had never felt so powerless. It wasn't a feeling Tori handled well.

In the next instant, he was stepping around her and into the room, the barrier suddenly gone. Tori blinked but didn't take time to question it, assuming that was a "Go ahead." She took three or four hesitant steps after him, while Krim brought up the rear. Her patient was on the floor, shaking and panting, but his focus moved instantly to her escorts and she started at the feral hiss followed by ominous clicking that came from the back of his throat. He kept those wicked-looking teeth covered though, thank Gaia, else she might have ducked behind Aderus. As it was, Tori reflexively took two steps closer to him, and that crimson gaze was back on her. There were some tense seconds of silence and wordless exchanges, so Tori decided to speak first. She raised the pint she still held in her hand.

"Would it be okay for me to come near you?" she asked, her movements stiff and jerky as she looked between him and Aderus.

He murmured something in their language from the floor, glaring at Aderus, who leveled his own glare down on the male, along with a clipped guttural response and intimidating flash of teeth.

"He will not attack," Aderus translated, assuring her, though his sharp gaze never left the male.

Go time. This is what you wanted.

The adrenaline poured through her veins as she moved forward slowly, careful to not make any sudden movements. She was sure they could all hear her heart slamming in her chest. The thought suddenly popped into her head that this is what it must feel like to come face to face with a Bengal tiger.

Tori went down to her knees and sat back on her heels, putting herself level with him, before scooting the last few feet. She gave him a tremulous smile but left a good gap between them. Being this close didn't help the intimidation factor. He was about Aderus's size, though slimmer. And much less controlled. She hadn't thought they could be more terrifying, but here it was. Thankfully, he hadn't directed that ferocity at her. Yet. Instead he watched her with a gaze that alternated between wariness and interest, if she had to label it. He kept stealing glances at her exposed skin, just as before, and when she got close he lifted his chin.

"I'm glad you let me help you," she said, aware of his eyes following her every move as she tried to tear open a corner of the still-warm bag with her fingers. There wasn't much relating to blood and gore that made her squeamish anymore, she'd seen it all in her profession. But Tori did have to admit to being more than a little put off with the idea of downing a whole bag of blood like it was tomato juice. Just the thought of its tangy metallic taste had her stomach churning.

Tori glanced up to see him watching her pathetic attempts. More specifically, staring at her short, blunt nails. *Oh, for fuck's sake!* she thought, blushing furiously, as she finally just lifted the corner of the bag to her mouth and carefully tore a small hole with her teeth. She winced, not the most sanitary thing but... She reached out, handing him the bag while being careful not to squeeze and spill its contents.

The pale Demon's gaze had been fixed on her mouth, but when she held out the blood, it moved immediately to the small red bag. His nostrils flared and in the next instant he had the bag to his lips, draining it in five seconds flat. Tori's brows rose as a strange half-hum, half-purr started from his chest.

She didn't have time to observe much else though. A rough tug on her arm pulled her through the air and out into the hallway before she even realized what was happening. Her head spun from the quick and abrupt change in position. It was amazing someone so large could move that fast, she thought, as she stumbled to catch her footing. The whole thing had probably taken less than two seconds and Aderus had released her immediately. Krim was along the wall to her left, and they stood out of direct sight of the room. Tori could still hear the humming though. She turned to Aderus, who was looking at Krim.

"What is that sound?" she asked, genuinely curious.

Not surprisingly, she never got an answer.

Chapter Eight

Tori dragged herself through the door to her temporary quarters aboard the *Amendment*. She was beyond exhausted, completely drained from the day's events, though it was barely evening. She wished she could have kept going. It wasn't every day you got the chance to be a liaison to the first extraterrestrials known in existence, but she wouldn't be of use in her current condition much longer. She'd already been coming off a double this morning, running on maybe four hours sleep in the last seventy-two, and was grateful she'd been allowed a time-out to recharge.

Something had definitely seemed off when she'd returned, though. Tori later discovered it was due to the fact Wells had tried approaching Jadar about letting the rest of the doctors help treat their wounded. After Aderus had firmly refused.

She wanted to slap her forehead in disgust.

Goddess help them if this was how Earth governments were going to play things. Tori would put in a good word for Delia, she decided. If she remembered correctly, the anesthesiologist also dabbled in hematology, which could be very useful considering what she'd learned today. She also felt they'd feel less threatened by smaller, human women. Anyway, she personally liked Delia. She was extremely even-tempered and perceptive, always listening before contributing sound, logical advice. On the job, she was no-nonsense and professional, but she also had a morbid sense of humor that Tori loved.

She sighed and plopped into one of the plush chairs in the small sitting area off the kitchenette. The hour-long debriefing with Wells and the other officials had started out as more of an interrogation, but Tori insisted she'd seen nothing of consequence, other than a brief glimpse at some technology she hadn't the expertise to explain, or comprehend. The ambassador and two others had quietly stepped out after a time and the rest of it had gone smoothly, if not uneventfully.

She told them nothing of the Demon's need for blood, though a battle raged in her head. The whole concept was disturbing, but a direct threat? She wasn't sure and didn't want to think so. She had told Wells she would report anything menacing or dangerous, but Tori knew the second that happened fear would start to rule over logic, which was when things always turned ugly. She understood they had trusted her with some extremely sensitive information and could just imagine how *not* well it would go if she didn't figure out how to explain it delicately to the higher-ups.

In the end, the fact that Aderus hadn't hurt or pressured her—*she* had been the one to volunteer her blood aboard their ship, no one else—made Tori resolute in her decision to keep her mouth shut until she could decide the best course of action.

One thing was pretty certain: Earth governments were switching tactics. She knew it from the look on their faces when Wells and the other two left the room earlier and it made her anxious.

Tori winced as she reached up to rub the knotted muscles at the base of her neck. Right now, she just wanted a hot shower, some food, and about 10 hours sleep. She took her time, staying under the steamy spray until her muscles relaxed and her skin turned pink. She brushed her damp hair up into a clip and found some clean scrubs in the linen closet to sleep in.

They always kept the quarters near the Med Ward stocked with basic sizes. She then padded out to the small kitchenette and dialed up a veggie stew on the food printer, which she ate in silence. By time she finished, she felt ten times better. Now all she needed were a few solid hours of sleep so good it feels like a coma and she'd be good to go.

Tori replayed the entire day in her head. It still felt surreal, like she couldn't quite bring herself to believe all that had happened in less than twenty-four hours. Earth's first real contact with extraterrestrials, the fact that they resembled some sort of... demonic-looking elf creatures. Tori barked out a laugh.

Her comm suddenly went off, pulling her from her thoughts, and the display in front of her lit up with a blonde-haired, hazel-eyed image when she put the call on View.

"Oh, thank the Goddess!" Liv exclaimed, the tension leaving her face when she saw Tori sitting comfortably in the chair. "They notified me right after you got transferred, but I've been worried sick. Are you all right?"

Liv's advanced security clearance (a perk of working aboard the *Phoenix*) coupled with the fact that she was Tori's only listed emergency contact and next of kin meant they would have contacted her discreetly, but with only the barest of details. "Hey. Yeah, I'm fine. No worries."

"Please tell me the rumors are true. Because if that's the case, I hate your ever-loving guts right now, I'm so fucking jealous."

Tori chuckled at her best friend's completely serious expression. "Um, I'm not entirely sure I know what you're talking about, but if I did I'd have to respond, 'No comment.'"

"I knew it!" Liv squealed as Tori's grin widened and she outright laughed.

She and Liv had always shared a passion for the stars, which was why when she chose her career path, astro-medicine had been the only option. Working to help people on board a huge ship that traveled the solar system, seeing other planets, imagining the beings that could occupy such planets and others like them—what could be more amazing? And Liv thought just like her. Up until today, it was the stuff of dreams. Now, Tori had to refrain from pinching herself again just to confirm that wasn't the case.

"I went crazy when I heard, but I'm really glad you're okay, honey," her best friend said, looking her over with a concerned gaze. "Still *so* jealous though. I knew you'd eventually find a way to make me regret not staying in med school with you."

"Yep, that's exactly how I planned it all along."

Liv slowly grinned, her hazel eyes sparking with excitement. "So, what can you actually tell me?"

Tori had done her best to remain calm and professional all day. Even in the face of how damn intimidating they'd been. But now that she had a chance to catch her breath, to reflect on the events of the past few hours, she felt like a kid on Christmas. She drew her legs up, hugging her knees.

"Well. They definitely take some getting used to..." Liv sat on the edge of her seat, lips parted, hanging on every word. Tori entertained her with a general description, then went on to tell Liv about the Demon's aversion to touch and about some of the sounds she'd heard them make. She talked about Jadar and Krim (though she didn't use names), giving brief descriptions, and even mentioned an "injured male" she helped treat. Tori was careful to keep things vague. She remembered from their briefings the type of information she was allowed to share and that any and all contacts would be closely monitored themselves.

"So, when are you getting me over there? You're my in, you know that, yes? I fully expect you to do whatever's necessary. Blackmail, knee pads, giving up your first-born child."

Tori laughed, shaking her head. "I'll see what I can do, but I can't promise anything. You'll just have to live vicariously through me till then."

"You *better* keep me posted."

"Yes, Mom."

"Okay." Liv sighed with a wistful look then rubbed her forehead tiredly. "I have an early appointment tomorrow and you look beat."

"What's wrong?" Tori frowned.

Liv waved her off. "Things have been driving me nuts lately, but I'll tell ya about that fun-tastic ball of crap later. By the way, I need your medical expertise. How long can a woman go without sex? Like, before her girl parts shrivel up and become nonexistent? I'm afraid when I finally meet someone worthwhile I'll open my pants and 'Poof!' Like a dry fart."

"I can't believe you just said that," Tori uttered flatly and covered her eyes, but her lips were quivering. "Love you!" she sang out to end the conversation before her friend could say anything more on a monitored call.

"Love you too." Liv winked. "Night."

Tori was still smiling as the view screen went black.

Chapter Nine

Aderus strode through the vessel *Amendment*, Jadar ahead of him and the male that called himself Vepar to his right. Humans led the way. Though strapped down with weapons, it was clear their movements lacked any predatory grace. They were meeting with a council of Earth's most powerful governments to "discuss terms."

One of the humans looked back, his eyes shifting nervously, and Aderus softly clicked his claws. It was something he did when anxious, the small motion helping to distract him. They knew this encounter would not just be about arranging materials for their damaged vessel. Earth's leaders would want to negotiate, and his kind did not like to be pushed. If one wanted to give you something, they gave it, and that was that. Askari were fiercely independent, aggressive...and that was just their males. Females were a whole other breed, made some of their males seem tame in comparison. Especially during breeding. When a female began to cycle, she attacked a male of her choosing. They were most aggressive then, aside from harboring young. The most deadly Askari alive was a harboring female. Even if the youngling was a male's own offspring, he couldn't come anywhere close. Aderus wondered passingly if human breeding was in any way similar. Reason told him not, given the frailty of the *doctor*.

The party escorting them stopped abruptly in front of a large entryway. His eyes flashed to Jadar and Vepar, reinforcing what ultimately mattered—getting what they needed from this isolated little world, so they could get back to saving their people.

He had a feeling it would mean going against their every instinct.

***

"You must understand, we're proposing an alliance. I suppose you could view it as a mentor-type relationship, but we're offering you access to every resource we have, as a planet and as a system…"

They stood facing a group of high-ranking Earth representatives, along with faces of a few dozen more on screens lining the wall behind them. They had tried to get them to sit when they entered, to no avail. Sitting surrendered power, and for Askari it was all about perception.

They had been trying to convince them to accept aid in the form of an "alliance" between Earth and Askara. Humans and Askari, working together, they said. More like humans demanding access to their technology in exchange for what they desperately needed to repair their vessel. He barely refrained from baring his teeth, and the more time that passed without a response, the more tense it became.

A new voice spoke then. Aderus's gaze moved to an older-looking male. He had been quiet up until now and wore a different uniform from the rest, closer to what the soldiers wore, but more elaborate. His short silver tresses were cut close to his head and the male held his gaze unflinchingly.

"Let us work with you, teach us what you know…" he said slowly, as if choosing his words. "And together, we'll build a whole damn armada of ships. We'll fight beside you, to help save your planet."

Aderus stirred, his golden gaze briefly finding Jadar and Vepar. This, they had not expected. Humans were in no way what he considered battle-worthy, but they had never had a race offer to fight *for* them.

Their war with the *Maekhurz* had been waging for many revolutions. The *shktal-llez* creatures were well known throughout the universe as world-killers and yet, not once had another race offered such aid. To be fair, they would not have accepted it, but circumstances had changed. They had been so proud, so sure of victory in the beginning. Now? They were so very close to being lost completely.

It was about more than just their home world, he thought, a dull ache in his chest. It would be as if they never lived, wiped from all of existence.

The older male spoke again. "I know you must not think much of us," he said in the same low tone. "Compared to you we're weak, far less advanced. But human lives are not something we take lightly." He looked between each of them. "We fight beside you, we die beside you. That's what we're offering here."

The silence in the room grew as they waited for some type of response. Aderus was skeptical, hesitant, but the more he quickly considered all aspects of such a pact, the more he began to believe it their best chance of returning home, even possibly saving their world. It would be unprecedented; Askara working closely with an off-world species, relying on them. They would have to teach the humans their technology. Then there was dealing with the cultural and biological differences. If an

Askari lost his temper he could easily kill a human with one blow. They were not known for their reserve.

They would have to learn, he decided. To survive, a species either adapted or died, and Aderus recognized they were at this pivotal point. This system was completely undiscovered, its resources untouched. A quick calculation told him Earth and its sister planets might have all the materials they would need. By forming an alliance, in Askara's name, they would gain access to them and a willing, if not inferior, fighting force. None of them had the authority to form such contracts, but they were the only ones representing their race. A fighting force of humans and Askari was better than what they had left—one last stronghold on Askara that would soon fall and a few scattered pockets of resistance within their planetary system.

They would build the strongest, most equipped vessels possible and the humans would gain what they wanted in the process. His hope grew.

Aderus realized then that perhaps he had been too quick to judge this planet and its people. True, they were not physically impressive, but they were tenacious. He sensed they would learn quickly and no other race had offered what they did. These Earthlings were willing to risk their lives for a fight that was not their own, a novelty Aderus respected greatly. He looked back to the silver-haired male.

"Your offer is generous, and we appreciate what you are willing to give. But we must discuss it with the others before we can answer you."

"Certainly. That's to be expected," a dark-haired official replied. "Take the time that you need. But know we cannot respectfully move forward until we can come to an agreement."

Aderus bristled at the soft-spoken threat and again leashed the urge to bare his teeth. This was going to be difficult. But they would convince the others to do what was necessary for the sake of their species. Earth and Askara would become allies.

Chapter Ten

Tori stretched and yawned, hip propped against the counter, as she waited for coffee. It was morning, her least favorite time of day. Although, on the ship everything was artificially controlled. She wished for the millionth time she could be like one of those people who sprang awake ready for the day, but the powers that be just didn't see fit to wire her that way. Waking up was a painful process, like coming out of a coma. Her brain usually needed a good hour to warm up, which made whenever she was on call especially fun. Liv loved to call her *Murphy*, after Murphy's Law, because anything she could possibly trip, fall or stumble over, she usually did. It was comical to everyone else, but after two trips to the ER as a patient, when she should have been showing up fit to work, it was downright annoying.

This morning was probably the closest she'd ever come to being "chipper." It only took a single memory of the previous day's events and she was on her feet with a shot of excitement. Tori had quickly found the bathroom, splashed some cool water on her face, brushed her teeth and drew her hair up into a loose ponytail before padding out to the kitchenette to grab something to eat.

"Port-side panorama," she said aloud to the room's computer as she held a toasty mug between her fingers. Hazelnut coffee with extra cream and sugar, Heaven in a cup. The large wall facing her faded away to reveal a stunning view of Earth. Tori frowned. They must have moved farther out as a precaution.

Though most of humanity accepted the concept of intelligent extraterrestrial life, people were still very much in shock—confused, afraid, at the very least wary. There were also isolated pockets of the population that hadn't matured as much socially. Places where modern-day stability and ideals had only recently taken hold, so the threat was a very real one. Tori hadn't seen the news in the last 48 hours but was sure there were small groups of fanatical morons protesting with calls of "The Apocalypse is here! Kill ET!!" or some such nonsense.

She thought back to her encounter with Wells yesterday as she sipped from her mug. She understood why the ambassador was pressing so hard. Any intelligent people, whether intent on war or peace, would want to know exactly who and what they were up against. She just didn't want to reveal any of the details she had learned until emotions cooled and everyone was thinking more rationally. She needed to consider both sides here.

Tori jumped as her comm went off and chose to answer it without View. "Davis here."

"Dr. Davis, its Ambassador Wells. I was told you were off duty, resting, so I waited as long as I could, but there have been some major developments and we must speak with you. I apologize for the short notice, but we're on our way to your quarters now."

"We?" Tori asked in surprise, looking down at the scrubs she'd slept in.

"Yes," the ambassador replied. "I am with Representatives Aderus, Jadar and...Vepar, whom I don't believe you've met. We should be there shortly. I'd say five minutes?"

Her heart raced as she scrambled to throw her mug in the washer and ran to the bedroom for her bra and a clean set of scrubs.

"Uh, okay, yes. Five minutes. See you then," she tried to say calmly but was sure it came out a little breathless.

"Shit, shit, shit!" Tori chanted as she ran around the bedroom like a madwoman, tearing her top over her head and frantically struggling with her bra. She turned to grab some socks and tripped over a shoe. She cursed, quickly pulling herself off the floor, and jammed her legs into some clean scrub bottoms, hopping around on first one foot then the other. The door chimed, and she lost her balance, slamming her right shoulder into the wall. Tori wrestled on a clean top and stole a quick glance in the mirror. She made a whining sound in the back of her throat. Her hair was mussed, her cheeks flushed, and she didn't have an ounce of makeup on. At least her skin still had that soft morning glow. She looked down at her bare feet as the tone sounded a second time. "Screw it," she mumbled, hurrying out to the kitchenette.

"Sorry, you can come in!" she called, disengaging the lock with the voice command.

Wells was the first to enter, followed by Aderus. The heavy locks at his temples dipped forward as he ducked into her quarters. Having him here, in her personal space, felt like all the air had left the room. He stood, observing his surroundings. Molten eyes met hers then dropped to her toes, poking out from under her pant legs. She scrunched them self-consciously then looked between him and Wells. "Sorry. I slept late and was still getting myself together when you called."

"That's quite all right. I apologize again for the short notice, but I'm sure you understand." Wells said distractedly, looking behind Aderus.

"Of course." Tori said, following his gaze. There were others and she moved a few steps back to give them room to enter. She clasped her hands briefly, wondering what was going on. What was so urgent that they had come to her personal quarters? Guess she'd find out soon enough, she thought with no small amount of apprehension. Tori looked over to the sitting area. The oversized plush chairs, arranged in a circle, should accommodate them all, but the low table in the middle would have to go, so she went to move it. She shuffled a few steps and set the table down carefully, out of the way. As she straightened, a familiar heat came up behind her.

Tori turned, having to look up to meet his gaze.

"You are smaller," Aderus rumbled.

"Yeah? Well, the shoes add an inch or two," she said, looking down and wiggling her toes.

His focus moved to her hair and she reached up to self-consciously finger her messy ponytail. She usually wore her hair pulled neatly into a bun at the back of her head.

"Dr. Davis, I believe you know Jadar, their medical specialist," Wells said as he came over to join them, the large mahogany-haired male directly behind him.

"Yes, I do. Hello again," she said with a small smile, meeting his green-eyed stare above the ambassador's head.

A third one stepped out from behind Jadar and locked gazes with her. Recognition hit—it was the one from their ship that had been working in the debris. Orange eyes. His stare took her in and then he advanced, startling her by moving closer. She had to force herself not to step back as he came to stand in front of her.

"Hi. Nice to meet you. I'm Tori."

He studied her silently before answering, "Vepar."

"It's nice to meet you, Vepar."

He flustered her to the point she had started to raise her hand in greeting, before she remembered herself and lowered it again. He seemed to have caught the gesture, though, because he rumbled something to Aderus over her head, to which the other male responded.

To her complete surprise, he slowly extended his hand. It took Tori a moment to reciprocate, but she carefully grasped his larger one. "Like that," she said with a small smile as she moved his hand up and down twice before letting go. Or trying to. He wasn't releasing her hand, she realized, looking down. Then a low clicking erupted behind her—damn sound gave her the chills—and he let go. Tori rubbed her arm.

"How about we all sit down?" she said anxiously, turning to the ambassador, whose sharp brown eyes missed nothing, as he carefully moved to one of the chairs. Tori noticed Aderus watched as she took the seat next to Wells before he moved to take the one on her other side.

The three large aliens exchanged uneasy glances before slowly lowering to sit. Even the large plush chairs were a tight fit, but she didn't hear the groan of reinforced alloy giving way so that was a good sign.

Aderus's ears pulled back. "It is...soft." Tori realized she couldn't remember seeing any real furniture on her visit aboard their vessel. The few surfaces she had glimpsed were smooth, hard metal, like the exam table. Then again, she hadn't seen any living quarters either, which led her to wonder what those would be like.

She chuckled, looking to the ambassador. "I guess we like things comfortable."

"Yes, well." The ambassador waved impatiently, leaning forward in his seat. "As I was saying earlier, there have been some very major developments in the past few hours and that's what we're here to talk to you about. Your role, anyway. This is extremely privileged information, as I'm sure you're aware, but, at this moment, Earth and Askara are in the midst of negotiating an alliance."

Tori stared, speechless.

"As you can imagine, it is something we very much wish to go successfully," Wells said earnestly, looking to Aderus.

This was a complete shift in thinking. The governments had been wary, untrusting, pushing for information. Now they were forging an alliance? Did they think it was the only way to keep Earth safe? Or simply the easiest way to get what they wanted? Not that Tori wasn't all for it. An alliance was beyond exciting. To think of the possibilities.

"We're very close to reaching an agreement, which is where you come in," the ambassador continued, interrupting her thoughts.

"Me? How exactly can I be of service?" Tori said warily.

"We essentially need you to play me, Doctor. They need a unanimous decision from all aboard their ship to enter into this agreement, but many have not met a human yet. Representative Aderus has voiced his preference that you be that person. Seems you've made quite the impression."

Tori's wide eyes found Aderus's ethereal stare.

She didn't quite know what to think. They'd given no indication they thought so highly of her. She might have been the only one they'd allowed aboard their vessel so far, but Aderus had still ended their liaison rather abruptly yesterday.

"Of course. I'd be honored," she said dazedly.

"Excellent! Then it's settled." The ambassador clapped his hands with a wide smile and stood. "We have every faith in you," he added, and it was then Tori realized the full implications of the role she'd just accepted. Her stomach dropped, and her shoulders suddenly felt very heavy.

This alliance would be all on her.

Chapter Eleven

Tori stood at the south gate of the *Amendment,* which connected directly to the Demon—*Askari,* she reminded herself for the tenth time—vessel. The ambassador was at her side, talking to other heads of state via his comm. She didn't want to think about that, though, because it would only make her more nervous. Instead she fiddled with the strap of the supplies tote that hung from one shoulder and tried not to fidget as her torso grew numb from the six pints of rapidly thawing synthetic blood she had secured around her back and belly. Though her position gave her unlimited access to the ship's medical supply room, it'd been trickier than she thought slipping away undetected.

She knew after she'd had time to think, however, that it was the right thing. She remembered what Aderus had said—there were more injured Askari that needed blood to heal. What better way to make a good first impression? Plus, Tori was a healer; she *needed* to help them. But what about the fact it was synthetic? She really hoped that wouldn't be a problem. Almost all blood for transfusions was synthetic now. What she'd done aboard their ship was old school. Besides, if it was good enough for the human body, it'd be good enough for them, right?

Tori looked up as the hiss and pop of the outer door signaled their arrival. Aderus stepped through and she could make out two others behind him, waiting on the other side of the gate. She greeted him with a smile and an anxious "Hello."

The soft, blue-green pulses of the walls calmed her as they entered, until she remembered the dreaded Decon chamber.

She stood stiffly beside Aderus, Krim and Vepar at their backs, willing it to be over and steeling herself against the horrible skin-crawling sensation. She watched Aderus's claws twitch.

"You may touch me," he said in low dual tones, startling her. Tori looked up and swallowed, knowing that it would help but also that he was far from thrilled.

"Thank you," she whispered and reached out. She gripped his forearm lightly, waiting for the party to start, and silently berated herself. Tori didn't want to continually appear weak in front of them. As her briefing hours before had made clear, she was to be a first impression for mankind. And that deserved better than her irrational fears.

As they exited the chamber, numbness around her torso quickly reminded her of the pints.

"I brought something," Tori said, stopping, and reached discreetly into her jacket and underneath her top. She pulled on the tab to release the fastener and the bags tumbled into her arms.

"I snuck into the supply room," she said, holding them up. "They're frozen synthetic blood. The heat from my skin should have thawed them enough to use by now... I hope the fact it's synthetic won't matter. Our bodies can't tell the difference."

The three looked between one another with unreadable expressions. Aderus was first to speak.

"Do your leaders know this?"

"Oh, no," Tori replied. "I haven't told them anything yet. I didn't think it wise until things calm down a bit and everyone is thinking more rationally."

"What would happen if they discovered it?"

"That I took the pints? Well, I guess the cat would be out of the bag. I'd have to explain why I took them. And I'd probably be in a whole lotta trouble. But I'm hoping that won't happen for a while. I blocked the feeds and adjusted the logs."

Tori couldn't tell whether he was stunned, suspicious or grateful as she stood patiently holding the pints.

"So, can you use them?" she prompted.

He carefully took them from her, holding all six in one hand, and pierced a small hole with one claw to test the liquid, as he'd done before. She watched him roll the taste in his mouth.

"Yes."

"Oh good," Tori breathed, her face lighting with relief.

"...*tahkaveen.*"

Tori's brows drew together. The word was uttered just as he turned away and, as they were of his alien tongue, she had no idea what he'd said. But she recited it in her head as she followed him down the corridor, determined to commit it to memory.

***

Aderus felt the weight of stares as those that were uninjured lined up for their first glimpse at the Earth diplomat sent to "make their acquaintance," as the humans termed it. Ears perked, and nostrils flared as they tried to pick up her scent.

Askari were innately curious and Tori was a contradiction.

Females didn't walk flanked by males. In truth, one would have viciously put him in his place, through tooth and claw, for the grave insult their behavior implied—only invalids, younglings and criminals received such treatment. They were fierce, unforgiving, controlling. You didn't approach one unless she welcomed it. But Tori was different, and the fact the *khurzha* wouldn't fight if one of them came closer might be enough for some to want to try it.

His gaze flicked back as she greeted each male they passed in some way. Again, something alien to them. Females purposely ignored males, unless they were cycling, or one did something especially impressive to gain her interest. Males regularly competed for that brief attention because it increased the chances she'd seek him out when it was time. Not that it happened much anymore. Their species did not cycle under extreme stress, which is what their very existence had been for many *sols* now. A dull-toothed, stub-fingered Earther was a poor comparison; the former of which she flashed frequently in what her kind called a "smile." So strange: to bare one's teeth in *greeting*, he thought, sensing some of the others were just as put off by it.

But despite her thin form and flat, compact features, Aderus acknowledged there was something about the fact she relied on him that...drew him. He didn't examine it any further than that. Instinct ruled them heavily, so such feelings were given great respect. He simply had to trust that on some level it was meaningful to their survival. And as he thought about what they might gain in an alliance with her people, Aderus realized for the first time that he couldn't help but feel grateful for their lack of females, though many aboard held a quiet rage that they had not been able to free some of them during their escape.

Memories of his captivity tried to surface, but he ruthlessly pushed them down. He would not dishonor Askara's most revered warriors by thinking of them as helpless captives at the mercy of their enemy, who seemed to derive a perverse pleasure from imprisoning and torturing their fiercest fighters. In truth, the escape of their small group had been the result of pure chance, a rare solar flare from their small sun that temporarily disabled their enemy's technology.

He remembered looking out as the barriers holding himself and those adjacent him imprisoned in cells no bigger than *swarktzha* dens had suddenly dropped. The looks of shock, restrained hope, then lethal determination as they realized the cosmos had blessed them with a rare opportunity. Even so, they had barely made it out alive. There was no question that if they hadn't been forced to *ssvold* to escape being destroyed, they'd have gone back to free as many as they could. But Aderus knew how much harder it would be for them now if females were among them—far more aggressive, far less restrained. This *alliance* would require a level of control that was foreign to them and would be a struggle instilling within himself. Let alone battle-hardened females.

***

Tori tried to keep pace as they strode through the halls of the alien vessel. Aderus silently led the way as she politely acknowledged any that she saw—her duty as emissary to a potential ally alien race. Or so she assumed.

She wasn't cut out for this ambassador business, though. She didn't like drawing attention to herself or the feeling of being under a microscope. She again reminded herself of the importance of this role, the immense honor and privilege she had been given—something other people would no doubt kill or die for—as she forced out another small smile in greeting. Still, she'd be happy when she was back aboard the *Amendment*, back to what she knew and did best. It made her think of how she'd rather be checking on patients; the injured male from yesterday, in particular. She wanted to know how he was doing and voiced as much to Aderus.

His back straightened, and he stopped, causing Tori to do the same or tumble into him. Then he actually spoke to Vepar and Krim without turning his head. Tori's eyes darted between the three of them. The conversation was brief but there was definite tension. She frowned, wondering why.

"This way," he rumbled, and she followed, struggling to keep up as they back-tracked to a familiar-looking corridor. She didn't miss the fact that a few of the others followed, seemingly not content to let the freakish human woman out of their sight.

Tori instantly recognized the "exam room" they passed from her first visit and a tingle of excitement ran up her spine. Aderus was going to allow her to follow up with him.

"Thank you," she voiced to his back, wanting him to know how grateful she was, and he turned his head in acknowledgement that she had spoken. Was he doing well? Had her blood healed him? She hoped so. How exactly did that work? Now that she'd had time to process it, she'd really like to know more about their biology. Yeah. Her and every other colleague.

As they came upon the room, Tori noticed there was no barrier in the doorway, as evidenced by the lack of a periodic light green shimmer. It was something she remembered in retrospect being present, then not, when they had entered the room before.

Her patient was sitting on a table, or sleeping platform. His back was against the wall, so he was facing them, legs bent with his arms resting on his knees. Tori could see he had new clothing and was dumbfounded as she took in his condition. This could not be the same individual she helped treat yesterday. It just wasn't possible. The milky white, unmarred skin of his forearms was easily visible and vicious-looking, hooked black claws graced his fingertips. Her eyes traveled over his face and now-clean locks. As with his arms, not a sign of injury. Where there had been deep, gaping wounds, there was only intact, unblemished skin. His head hung down, eyes closed; he appeared to be resting, a fact she took advantage of as she finished her quick visual inspection. They'd been present no more than a couple of seconds, however, before that ominous clicking sounded from within the room, ending on a deep-throated hiss. Tori felt the skin of her arms tighten with goosebumps. He knew they were there. His nose twitched, and his eyes opened, dark red irises meeting her own.

Tori pushed back a feeling of unease and smiled. While stunned at his condition, she was very glad he was doing so well. Her contribution had healed him.

"Hello there. Do you remember me? From yesterday?" she asked, taking a cautious step forward.

As if her movement was the trigger, he bolted from the table, his body moving so smoothly it was almost as if he floated. She felt Aderus tense. He stood ahead of her, blocking half the entrance to the room, but the male moved within inches of them, his gaze completely trained on her. Her smile faltered. Vepar stood next to her on the right, but Tori instinctively knew as long as she stayed behind Aderus, she'd be all right. Her throat moved on a swallow. The male didn't take his gaze from her as the tension grew. Aderus's eyes were ablaze as they focused on him and she watched his upper lip curl back to reveal his teeth. Tori's stomach dropped; this didn't look good. Whether conscious of it or not, she took two steps closer to Aderus, which seemed to provoke a response from the male. Aderus countered with a threatening step to the right, blocking him from her even more. This time the eerie clicking and hissing came from him, the air practically vibrating with it, and she stilled in dreaded anticipation.

She did not want to see a fight between these two. She did not want Aderus injured protecting her. The thought made her sick. *Where the hell was the barrier?!*

There was an explosion of movement, as if her panicked thoughts had caused a string to snap. Tori stood frozen as she watched Aderus throw his body into the other male and they both went flying back into the room. Literally flying. The floor beneath her feet vibrated with the impact as the two of them hit the wall. Then it was brutality in its purest form. No nature exclusive could have prepared her for the sheer viciousness of watching them fight. It was like watching trains collide. The sickening sounds of muscle and flesh pounding against one another, then the tearing of said flesh as they ripped into one another with teeth and claws. Tori stood watching in horror. It was hard to make out who was where one moment to the next, partly because they moved so quickly and partly because of the dim lighting, black walls, and dark uniforms, but the red-eyed male's light skin stood out enough she could tell when he had

Aderus pinned and was about to deliver a brutal, possibly fatal bite to his throat. *No!*

She looked desperately to Vepar and Krim, but they were just standing there, *watching. What the fuck?! They're just going to stand there and let this happen?! What is* wrong *with them?!*

A recklessness tore through her and the next thing Tori knew she was running into the room. By some miracle, she ducked Vepar's arm and launched herself at the pale male. "NO!" she shouted, as she pushed at his face and shoulders with all her strength, using her forward momentum to swing herself onto his back. Tori wrapped one arm around his neck and the other over his eyes, hanging on for dear life as he reared back with a bone-chilling hiss. She felt a crushing grip on her shoulder, a hot, searing pain on her arm and then she was sailing through the air, crying out as she hit the floor and slid to make contact with the wall. Hard.

The first thing she felt was pain. A lot of it. *Please don't let anything be broken*, she thought, battling between the urge to stay still and to crawl out of the way. Her ears rang, and her vision was blurred, but she could hear the deep-throated hisses and snarls in front of her. A large mass went flying across the room. She felt the vibrations when he hit the floor and then again when a darker-colored mass landed on top of him to slam what she assumed was a head brutally into the ground, because after that, the light-colored blob stopped moving. Relief coursed through her.

Tori closed her eyes, her face contorting in agony. Her hand was wet. Shit. The entire arm of her white coat was drenched in red.

She felt movement and glanced up to see who she assumed was Aderus crouched over her; gold eyes. His head shot around, and harsh sounds left his mouth, heavy locks almost hitting her face with the movement. Wetness on her thigh drew her attention again and she looked down. She was bleeding out, fast. The crazed male must have ripped open a vein, or worse, an artery. Tori glanced around, fumbling. "My pack," she croaked. The next thing she knew her medical pack was on the floor next to her.

"What do you need?" The deeply growled question was hardly understandable. She could tell she didn't have much time so didn't bother with an explanation as she stuck her good hand inside the pack. Tori fumbled around weakly in the bag, her body now shaking. She thanked Gaia when her fingers closed around what she was looking for and withdrew the tube of coagulant. Her breaths came fast and shallow and she could feel sweat dripping down the side of her face, but she pushed herself to jerk up the shredded sleeve of her now crimson coat, crying out at the pain it caused, to apply the gel thickly to her wounds. She managed to get ahold of the epo-injector in the pack's front pocket next and jammed that into her thigh as well. Then, knowing she'd done all she could, she collapsed back on the floor, breathing heavily. Her eyes drooped.

Aderus was rumbling something at her, a look in his eyes that could have been concern. She sensed others around her, caught flashes of color. Tori turned her head toward him again. Hardly aware of what she was doing, she inched the fingers of her injured arm along the floor and feathered them lightly over his fingers. A faint smile touched her lips. "Pretty," she murmured, just before her eyes closed.

Chapter Twelve

Aderus struggled to remain calm as he watched her unfocused gaze move about, the small female surrounded by a bright pool of her own blood. His chest heaved, partly from his fight with the *palkriv* and partly from his own terror. Yes, he was afraid. He had personally assured this human's safety; the success of the alliance between their two worlds depended on it. But he was unused to having to protect another. Definitely not a female. Why did she attack? What had she been thinking?!

He tried her name, chafing at the intimacy, but the little *khurzha* didn't seem cognizant. Her kind did not heal well, judging by how much blood coated the floor in so little time. It was everywhere, and he knew instinctually her life was in danger. Though whatever she had done seemed to have stopped the bleeding, they did not know what to do to ensure she survived. When he whipped his head around to again bellow for Jadar, he felt her fingers brush his own. Aderus jerked around in time to see her strange eyes slip closed. His blood turned cold. This human's death would most likely mean their own. In their disadvantaged state, they'd be no match for a planet even as primitive as Earth. Humans still possessed weapons capable of destroying them. More than that, Aderus had started to hope that they might have a future, that they might be able to take back their world.

Jadar finally appeared beside him, pushing to get closer. Under normal circumstances, it'd be enough to provoke aggression, but all of Aderus' focus was on the lifeless form next to him. He didn't move, the proximity making him able to detect her weak pulse. She was alive, but barely.

"What do we do?" he growled at the *khurzhev*.

The male's keen gaze moved quickly over her body.

"She injected something." Aderus told him.

Jadar moved with deadly purpose to the wall display, his fingers moving with more speed than grace. The silence was suffocating as they waited. A few from the main part of the ship stood watching in the corridor. Many did not yet know how to feel about their human hosts, but it was clear how condemning the situation could be.

"A blood-producing stimulant of some sort." The healer rumbled. "But she has lost too much to compensate on her own. Her heart is weak and erratic."

Aderus's brow rose a fraction as what he said registered. She needed blood? Then he remembered her saying humans transfused their blood and in the next instant he thought of what she had brought.

***

Sound was the first thing that came back to her. The quiet hum of a ship. Tori could feel the slight purr of it beneath her fingers. Her mouth felt like cotton and she swallowed hard. Pain was the next sensation; everything hurt. Her head throbbed, and her arm felt even worse. She rolled her head to the side. It felt like she was propped against a wall. Sensing movement next to her, she pried her eyes open. A dark form dominated her vision. Tori blinked several times and the picture came into focus. Un-earthly eyes. They blinked back at her.

"You wake. Are you well?"

Growled words, spoken in strange dual tones. They sounded oddly detached, though Tori sensed an impatience to them. She didn't feel quite lucid as her eyes drifted to take in her surroundings. The room seemed familiar... Then she started to recall everything that happened and groaned, looking down at her arm. Her coat was gone, and her scrubs were somehow clean. No sign whatsoever of her near-death experience, save the thick white bandage that covered the length of her forearm.

She tried to speak, ended up coughing and tried again. "W-water. Please."

Something was pressed into the hand of her good arm and she shakily raised it to her lips. She gulped the entire thing in one go, only noting afterward that it tasted different. Earthy. She opened her eyes as she finished the last drops to find Aderus crouched nearby, watching intently. There was a tic in his powerful jaw and his eyes almost glowed. She tried sitting up straighter but winced. The hard floor was murder on her already battered body. It was then she noticed a small mark on her inner arm.

"What happened?"

"We transfused you blood."

Shock washed over her, followed by relief, and finally, guilt. She was relieved they'd had the insight to transfuse her, likely saving her life. But she fretted over the fact they had had to use the synth blood she brought that had been meant for the others.

"Damn it," she said, closing her eyes. "I'm sorry."

He studied her, still crouched, one arm braced on the floor. "Why did you attack?"

Tori's eyes popped open. "Attack?" A frown marred her brow. "I was trying to help you. No one else was. He was going for your neck."

She watched his nose wrinkle and blazing eyes narrow. "I did not need help. And we do not interfere in each other's disputes."

Tori just stared at him, lips parted. "Disputes," she said slowly. If anything, she'd been expecting a thank you. Instead he seemed...irritated? Scolding? The telltale warmth of a blush graced her cheeks. She couldn't believe he was treating their brutal death match like some minor difference of opinion! But apparently, that's what it had been. And the reality of it was a slap to the face.

She almost laughed at the absurdity of the situation and had to try hard to keep her voice calm. "Well, *we* try to settle our—disputes—with*out* violence. And if it escalates to that, others try to stop it." She released a breath. She didn't have the energy to get upset and it wouldn't help anyway. "This just shows how much harder we're going to have to work at communicating if we want things to work. For my part, I'm sorry I assumed." She winced, adjusting her arm, then mumbled, "Anyway, I don't think the light-skinned one meant to hurt me; he just reacted." Tori still didn't know his name.

Aderus didn't reply as he stood, his fluid movements unlike any known creature. Tori watched as he ran a thumb claw across his other claws on the same hand, rhythmically. He wasn't looking at her, but instead seemed to be contemplating what she'd said.

Chapter Thirteen

Tori managed to keep her injuries hidden, which wasn't easy. She couldn't always pop pain meds when she was hurting and certainly not while she was on duty. But she'd had the insight to pack a long-sleeved undershirt in her tote that day which had helped to conceal the bandages when it came time to return to the *Amendment*. Aderus had seemed wary, even suspicious, that she was willing to cover what happened, but Tori knew it was the right decision. No matter how indifferent he acted, she sensed their desperation, and it made her want to do whatever she could to help them, even if she knew her job was the least she could lose. She knew no good would come of her superiors knowing the truth, not yet. And Tori felt like some serious progress had come out of the whole situation after all. When Aderus had asked how they could communicate better, she'd been thrilled. She told him they needed to learn more about one another, about the differences between Askari and human culture, so that they could interact better. Looking back, she had to stifle a laugh. It was like they didn't understand social basics.

Today, he walked her to a room off a different corridor. It was bigger than the others she'd seen. A common room maybe? She was about to ask, when the wall facing them morphed into one of the most stunning stellar landscapes she'd ever witnessed, and she gasped at the large planet that filled her vision to the right. It was as if they were actually in orbit around it—the swirling oranges and reds vividly surreal. A distant red star shown to the left.

"Wow, that is..."

"Our home," he rumbled beside her.

"That's Askara?" she asked, pointing to the large orange planet.

"That is *Kharhisshna*, our Mother Planet. That is Askara," he said, inclining his head toward what looked to be a modest dark moon. She studied his world, hungry to know everything she could. It was so different from Earth—no blue oceans or white clouds. Instead their home reminded her much of the pulsing black metal that comprised their ship. She could just make out jagged mountainous peaks beneath thick lavender clouds. Tori found herself wondering what it would be like to look up into mauve-colored skies.

"It's so different," she blurted.

"Different. And the same," he said in dual tones, surprising her by answering.

He stared almost longingly. The dark moon belonged to a planet thousands of light years away. It looked nothing like Earth. It was strange and alien and unreal...

Tori looked at Aderus then, viewing him in a way she hadn't before. A humanoid form: eyes, ears, nose, mouth—all the same as her. Even the equivalent of hair on his head. Sure, the details were different, but so what? He was right, she realized. Though she had a feeling he had probably been referring to their planets—er, moon. Whatever. She understood, and smiled.

"It's beautiful. I hope I can see it one day."

He flashed her a guarded look. She kept the smile in place.

"I appreciate you showing it to me." She waited for him to say something. More silence. Tori sighed.

"Look. I know talking isn't the primary way you communicate, but for humans, it's a big deal. It's how we get to know and understand one another. It's how we form connections. So, if you have questions about Earth, or us, or what I'm thinking—anything—just ask. I'll tell you honestly." She paused and gathered her courage. "For instance, if you had told me it was dangerous to visit the light-skinned male, that he was unstable and not contained, I wouldn't have pushed. I would have trusted your judgment and let it go."

"You would have yielded?"

"Of course." She nodded. "I know nothing of your ways, your behaviors. That's why I'll be asking a lot of questions. Which, for the record, is rude when you don't reply." He blinked with those extra lids and his quiet reflection didn't surprise her. What did, however, was the boisterous reply from her stomach as it chose that very moment to communicate its discontent. Tori quickly slapped a hand over her abdomen, flushing as another low rumble sounded from her midsection. She hadn't been eating as much in the morning the last few days because of nerves.

Aderus's eyes darted to her belly and it looked like he tensed as he heard the sound again, his clawed fingers curling slightly at his sides.

"That'd be my tummy telling me it's hungry," she explained.

Chapter Fourteen

Aderus eyed the small foodstuff in Tori's lap. She had asked him for some water, of which she questioned him on the receptacle. It seemed to fascinate her as she turned it over with short, clawless fingers. She must not have remembered the first one she drank from. It was made of the same material as their ship. The same precious metal that, as far as they knew, was scarcely found anywhere else but on Askara. It was their most valuable resource and the reason the *Maekhurz* attacked their world. They were the only beings to ever have dared take it by force since they had gone through their own *Dekhaveep* more than a millennium ago. The organic metal could take the shape and state of whatever one programmed of it, then disseminate just as fluidly. They used it for everything—their ships, their homes, their clothing. It had a life force unlike any living creature, one they had yet to fully understand. But that life constantly flowed through it in the form of soft blue-green pulses. It needed energy to grow, "food" in the form of various elements, of which this system had plenty. If they could get enough of what they needed, the vessel should be able to repair itself, with their guidance.

He told her none of this, of course. The humans would learn of Askara's great resource in time. Today, he was glad she had survived because it meant they still had a chance to save their world.

He had deactivated the stellar display while she rummaged through her pouch, then watched as she struggled to lift herself onto the seat opposite him.

She had said they needed to speak, to communicate better. He would not have listened to her before, but with what had happened, he was willing to try. They needed this alliance. And part of him realized how pitiful it was that he had come to see such a meek, naïve race as necessary to their survival, but that just attested to how desperate they were. Whatever the reasons, it was something he now clung to with everything he was because it was the only thing that gave him hope.

Aderus was unsure how to proceed, however. What did she want him to speak about? The notion was bizarre: talking for the sake of talking. No, that wasn't right. She said he should not hold back his thoughts or questions. He stared at her, watching her fidget and work at the wrapping encasing her foodstuff.

"Your stomach speaks when you are hungry?" he asked, inclining his head. That earned a huffing noise and flash of flat teeth as she glanced briefly up at him.

"I suppose you could say it that way."

"Is there pain?"

She looked back up and held his gaze, faint lines between her brows and a downturn to her lips. "Not really pain, no. But it can be painful once you reach the point of starvation, many days without food. Don't D—I mean, Askari, experience something similar?"

"If we are deprived of sustenance for too long our bodies go through a wasting. It is very painful."

Her eyes widened. "Oh. That's...horrific. Is it treatable?"

He *snikted* in affirmation. "Blood is needed more than food. A similar thing happens when we are injured."

Various expressions played across her face. One could almost feel the thoughts whirling through her mind.

"So, the ones I brought the pints for—that you had to use on me because of that whole... misunderstanding—are they?" His gaze locked with her strange eyes from beneath his brow. True to his kind, he hated to admit weakness, but it was something that weighed heavily on him since she'd recovered. He had been trying not to think of it but couldn't deny hoping she would find another way to get them more.

"Yes," was all he said.

She seemed lost in thought, the package of foodstuff all but forgotten in her lap. He inclined his head and sniffed. It smelled sickeningly sweet.

"Okay. I'm going to find a way to get you more."

Her voice was deeper, her tone authoritative, and he bristled at the way her blue and white orbs flashed in what could only be determination. It was the way he was used to a female behaving and for a brief moment, he allowed himself to see her as such.

"How much time, before it gets really bad for them?"

He thought a moment. "Three Earth days."

"And what happens after three days?"

"For some, death."

***

Tori tried to tamp down her growing restlessness as she digested the fact she had less than seventy-two hours to figure out how to get them more blood. If any of his kind became more ill or, Goddess forbid, died, she'd somehow feel personally responsible. She looked to Aderus and could only imagine how he must feel. Her fingers brushed the trail bar still lying in her lap.

"Would you like to try some?" she asked, looking for a distraction.

A thin upper lip curled back, and he leaned away, which she was pretty sure was the universal sign for disgust. Tori frowned. She considered their double rows of dagger-like teeth and an uneasy feeling came over her. The second set wasn't as visible. They hung above the first, protruding from the equivalent of their gums, but she'd gotten an eyeful on more than one occasion.

"Do you not eat plants?" she asked hesitantly.

The large Askari made a low *grumph*, and stood.

She watched as he moved to a spot on the wall behind him. His broad back was blocking most of what he was doing so Tori leaned to the side, trying to get a better view. He turned back with a black bowl-like thing. Perhaps she'd been imagining it, but no—there it was again! Definite movement; a writhing and whipping back and forth. She jerked, startled. It was hard to see clearly from her seated position, but as he approached she felt herself blanch. Her eyes finally locked on something over the edge of the bowl. They resembled large maggots, pale gray in color with long stiff black hairs, or at least, what she could see of them. Disgust churned her stomach something fierce.

Please don't tell me they eat those things... And he was turned off by my trail bar? Are you kidding *me?*

She shrank against the hard metal back of her seat as Aderus came closer. She didn't dare take her eyes off the creatures, their violent movements creating slapping and scraping sounds against the sides of the bowl. Bile unwillingly surged up her throat—she really hoped she was wrong about where this was headed. If so, it appeared they weren't going down without a fight. Aderus didn't look up as he resumed his seat across from her, hunching over the bowl.

"Are you—is that food?" she asked, trying to keep her voice even. They looked nearly as thick as her wrist.

"*Rukhhal.*"

Without another word, he stabbed one of the worms with his claws. Tori watched the creature thrash back and forth, trying desperately to escape, but what had her fingers moving involuntarily to her mouth was the sickening crunch, pop and squish as he chewed.

I think I'm gonna be sick, she thought, swallowing hard.

"Do you always eat them a-alive, or...?" she said weakly, trying to tune out the sound.

He blinked back at her, powerful jaw muscles working like crazy.

"Are your plant foods not alive until the moment you pick them? Food affords the most nutrients fresh."

Right. If their version of fresh was alive while chewing, then cooking was probably a travesty. She couldn't deny that what he said *did* give her a whole new perspective on her daily salads.

Tori tried to distract herself while he continued to eat. She thought about politely nibbling on her trail bar, but the thought of anything near her mouth made her want to vomit. Thank whatever deity they might believe in he hadn't offered her any.

He glanced down at her lap. "You are not eating."

"Erm, I will. I'm just resting," Tori replied lamely.

His penetrating gaze didn't waver. "I think you are disgusted by my food."

Tori blinked. Shoot. She had said she'd answer him honestly. "Well, yes. I was trying to be polite, but those things completely disgust me. I'm sorry." She swallowed. "I'll eat as soon as my stomach settles."

The large Demon made a throaty noise and continued eating, completely unaffected by what she said. He even watched her as he threw the next writhing maggot into his mouth. Tori tried to stop her eyes from fluttering at the sickening sound but failed. Then that noise—like a cross between a hum and someone clearing their throat. It wasn't the first time she'd heard it.

"What does that mean? That sound?" She had an idea, but what he just did seemed to confirm it.

He immediately glanced down, and the noise stopped. *Oh, no you don't.* She waited patiently, and finally he answered. "Most often it conveys, amusement."

He *was* teasing her! She let lose a genuine laugh, which she realized afterward was probably the first time she'd done so in front of him. He jerked, straightening, and even stopped chewing. Thank Gaia.

"That's how we show amusement, laughter," Tori said with a smile. "You were teasing me just now, gaining amusement from something you know makes me uncomfortable. We do it often. Though some people don't like it."

He relaxed slightly and resumed chewing, his eyes moving over her face. "What does it mean when your color changes?" He looked down to grab another...ugh, giant maggot...and this time Tori was the one fidgeting. She forced herself to hold his gaze even though she felt the telltale stirrings of heat. Sometimes just thinking about it brought it on. Though she was usually able to control it. He just flustered her.

"It's called blushing and signifies discomfort, for one reason or another. Not all people blush, but it's more noticeable with lighter skin."

Aderus finished the rest of his meal in silence and Tori couldn't help the silent prayer of thanks when he was done.

Chapter Fifteen

She decided the best way to get them more synth blood was to just block the feeds and adjust the logs again. According to the records, inventories were only performed once a month, so she had time to figure out how to deal with it. She managed to bring them six more pints and another four the day after that. Jadar seemed grateful and Aderus thanked her again using a new word. *Khurzha*.

When she asked him what it meant, he had told her "healer," and she inwardly beamed. Things seemed to progress well after that. Her arm was healing and Aderus talked to her a little more each day. On the fourth day, he reached across them, bridging the space. It took her a moment to realize he was trying to give her something—the tiny object held between his fingers, hidden by dark claws.

Tori slowly raised her hand. A tiny flat disk no more than an inch in diameter lay in her palm. The dark color and reflective property reminded her of their clothing.

"Place it on your skin."

Tori blinked at him, partly in awe and partly shocked that he would so willingly give her a piece of their highly coveted technology.

"Why would you give this to me? I mean, thank you, but..."

"It is tougher than flesh and absorbs impact."

"It'll help protect me," she finished, touched by the gesture. "That's—uhm. Thank you," she murmured again, peering curiously at her palm. "You know they're going to take this from me, right? They'll dissect it piece by piece."

"They will try," he replied cryptically.

She frowned and studied the little black coin.

"Do I just, put it anywhere?" Tori asked, turning it over in her hand. It was warm to the touch, which she couldn't tell was from him holding it or if that was its natural state. She got the strangest impression it was *alive* in some way. But that was crazy.

His fingers tapped the side of his neck, under his locks. "It is most common."

Tori had so many questions, but she didn't want to annoy him with a barrage. She had confidence he wouldn't give her anything that was harmful, but her breath still quickened. She was about to cover her skin with alien technology, something never seen or experienced anywhere on Earth. It both excited and terrified her. It was embarrassing to admit, but her first thought was how the thing would feel, or act, against her private areas. It stood to reason that if it followed along her skin it would expand beneath her clothing, even her underthings.

She slowly lifted the disk and placed it on the skin above her collarbone. Nothing happened. Tori realized she'd been holding her breath and released it in a puff, then frowned, looking to Aderus.

"Press once." He mimed.

Made sense, you had to activate it or something. She took another breath then reached up and gently pressed with her middle finger. Instant warmth flowed over her skin like water. It started from the disk and spread outward over her chest, shoulders, then down her arms and torso. It moved quickly, and she stiffened when she felt it cover her groin and backside but relaxed as she realized it wasn't intrusive in any way. If anything, it felt...supportive. Even her breasts beneath her plain cotton sports bra felt more secure. The warmth slid beneath her pants, down her legs and finally to her feet. Her shoes grew tight, so she reached down and removed them with a tug, followed by her socks. Tori studied her new footwear with wonder. They were an extension of what covered the rest of her body, with the exception that there was a stiffer, cushioned surface along the bottom, not unlike the tread of a shoe. The difference was that it conformed to her foot like it was made for it. She took a hesitant few steps. No shoe had *ever* felt this good. She was so ruined. Despite appearances, the material was quite breathable, too. Her whole body felt good. Warm. Light. Strong. She couldn't quite explain it but looked up to Aderus and flat-out grinned.

She took a few strides in a circle, an excited laugh escaping her. "This is amazing!" He watched as she spun and gave a little jump. Then she stopped and looked down the front of her shirt. It was very form-fitting, but the reflective property afforded some modesty. Her scrubs looked funny over top, she was sure, but she didn't remove them. Call her shy, but she wasn't that comfortable with the idea just yet. Tori couldn't stop playing with it, though, constantly running her fingers lightly over the material. She knew the *havat*, as Aderus said it was called, was going to cause a stir and worried she wouldn't be allowed to keep it.

That turned out to be somewhat of an understatement.

Back on board the *Amendment*, she was just as alarmed as the technicians when they found that the alien technology didn't seem to want to leave her skin. At first, she'd panicked. She had pressed on the small round disk multiple times, trying to get it to retract, and cursed her own stupidity that she hadn't bothered to check with Aderus as to how to deactivate it. She had just assumed the same action that activated it would deactivate it.

You know what they say about assumptions, Murphy. She could hear Liv's mocking tone.

What was more shocking, when they then tried to cut the thing from her body, it would respond with a pulse of blue-green light which seemed to bend or break every metal instrument that got close with the intent to do harm. Those pulses had felt strange against her skin. Electric, warm...*aware*. It was the same when they tried to scan the material. The instruments would suddenly glitch and it was then that she recalled Aderus's words from earlier.

They will try.

She had finally argued they stop. That she would just go to Aderus or Jadar. It was best it not be damaged in any way, though the ship's scientists were more than frustrated at a missed opportunity to confiscate Askari technology.

Only after she was escorted from Decon did she realize the bigger problem as her bladder chose to make its presence known. She almost cried in relief when she got to the bathroom and something told her to try pressing on it one more time to blessedly find it recede up her legs and groin so that she could relieve herself. Tori had sat playing with it for a while after that. She found she could get it to function just fine except for the fact she didn't know how to remove the disk itself from her skin. The little metal coin seemed permanently attached to the base of her neck, but for now she was just grateful she could use the facilities without having to go to one of them for help.

Talk about embarrassing. As best she could figure, it must go into some sort of "lock down" mode when confronted with a hostile environment.

When she asked Aderus how to remove it the next day, he looked at her strangely, but just the idea of something alien being stuck to her skin was starting to freak her out. Not to mention, washing. He had acted put off but showed her, and when she mimicked his fingers, nothing happened.

"It is not ready to release." He rumbled curiously.

"What do you mean, it's not ready? Aderus, I'd like this thing off me."

"It has linked to you."

"Are you saying you gave me some kind of parasite?!"

That earned her two clicks and a hiss. "Not a parasite."

"What then?"

"It will learn your body's responses, help you to adapt and react. Your heat gives it energy. You can move the *havat* once it senses you do not wish to remove it."

"So, it's...alive?"

"In its own way." Another cryptic answer. Tori didn't like it. There were things he wasn't telling her.

"You should have told me," she said flatly, more than a little irritated. "I thought we agreed on honesty."

His ears flicked. "I did not know. You are not Askari."

"You still should have told me how it normally works."

"The *havat* cannot harm you, it is good. That is why I gave it to you."

Aderus didn't seem to understand why she was making such a fuss and she'd been around him enough to tell he was getting irritated. So, she let it go with a sigh. This was a battle for another time and he did have a point. The way he'd said it made her feel she should be grateful.

Tori found her hands strayed to the material even more after that, not able to resist brushing her fingers lightly over the sleeves or at the neckline where it met her collarbone. She didn't realize she was doing it half the time. The idea had been scary at first, but after a few days she found the notion...comforting? Then the *havat* started to emit soft pulses every so often in response to her touch. It startled her initially, but now she smiled. She must be crazy, too, because she'd started to talk to it, especially when she was alone in her quarters at the end of the day. She'd even named it.

Henry. Tori snickered. It just felt like a *he*, though the concept didn't creep her out like she thought it would.

She wondered if all the Askari had a similar connection with the material that covered their bodies. She'd have to ask Aderus. Or maybe Jadar. Tori frowned as she sat off the kitchenette, sipping some herbal tea to unwind from another long but stimulating day.

She'd been working closely with Aderus for days now, playing liaison between Earth and the Askari, learning what she could, providing answers and insights. He would ask questions, she would answer. And vice versa. Sometimes he flustered her, despite her best efforts, and it wasn't that she blamed him. She was more irritated at herself. Blushing, fidgeting. What was wrong with her? Sure, some of the questions weren't delicate, but that was to be expected and she was a professional. Like, when he'd asked about *human breeding*. Her cheeks had flamed, and she'd tiptoed awkwardly around the answer, like a twelve-year-old. She didn't know any way to explain it, other than she'd become very aware of him lately. It was probably because of how much time she'd been spending around him. Plus, there was her fascination with anything space-related. So, it made sense, she supposed.

She'd started studying him a lot, noticing all the nuanced differences of their bodies. The Askari were humanoid in form, but their proportions were different. They moved differently, too, their limbs lean, lanky and lithe. His fingers were triple jointed, and what she would consider his pinky was stunted and protruded farther down, almost at the wrist. Like a vestigial digit. His wide-set eyes had transfixed her from the get-go, but the rest of his facial features were harsh, angular. His nose was snout-like, with nostrils set into his face, instead of outside it. Their lips were thin, barely concealing a double row of jagged teeth, and the upper had a slight split in the center. They were a shade darker than his skin.

Ever since he'd shown her his home world, however, Tori viewed their differences less as divisions and more as intrigues. The fact she had spent so much time watching his mouth when he spoke lately set off little warning bells in her head.

She did *not* have a—no! It was just curiosity. And it didn't matter. He sure as Gaia wouldn't, couldn't, see her in that way, so what was the point even having those thoughts. Right? Eventually, Tori got tired of arguing with herself and went to bed, but the next morning it was all she could think of. Like finally admitting it to herself had opened the floodgates. So, she squashed her reserve and left her quarters to meet Aderus scrub-less. It was just her and Henry today, she thought, brushing the sleeve lightly. She smiled as it emitted a soft pulse. The ship's scientists had given up. When she relayed to them what

Aderus had told her, their eyes lit with greedy fascination, but there was little they could do. She was restricted to either the Askari vessel or her quarters, under constant vid feed, for the next four weeks, but she understood the necessity for such protocols.

Aderus met her at the gate, along with Krim. His molten gaze swept quickly down her body and his nose scrunched once before he said something short to Krim. Tori didn't know what she had been expecting. Nothing but the *havat* covered their skin, so she had wanted to embrace it, be bold. But she'd be damned if she let anyone make her feel ashamed of her body. A part of her had wanted to see how Aderus would react to seeing so much of her true shape and now she knew.

She couldn't say she'd gone so far as to entertain the idea of what sex might be like with one of them—she wasn't sure that was even possible—but it was clear any stirrings of interest would not be reciprocated, and they had much more important things to worry about. As per Wells, the Askari would be meeting to finalize the conditions of the alliance any day now.

"I should tell you," she said as they entered the ship. "Speaking in your language around other humans will be perceived as rude because we can't understand what you're saying." It might have been a slight jab to make her feel better, but the point was true.

Krim walked beside her and she caught his blue-and-white-streaked gaze roaming her body. Her cheeks heated. Maybe it had been a mistake not wearing her scrubs today. She was drawing more attention to herself. It would help if Tori just knew what they were thinking when they looked at her. Especially as the day went on and she got more of those looks.

"What do your females look like?" she asked Aderus when they broke at midday to eat. He was hunched over a bowl of *rukhhal* again, completely absorbed in his meal. The room they were in turned out to be some sort of common area, but Askari rarely ate together, she'd learned. They were very solitary and could even be food aggressive.

He watched her for a few moments as he chewed. Tori had managed to tune out the sound enough that she could eat without it turning her stomach. He spoke then, and it registered that the two-toned hisses and growls were him communicating with what seemed to be a ship-based AI. A stunningly life-like hologram appeared in the fifteen or so feet that separated them and Tori started in surprise.

It was a female—at least that was what she assumed. Her lips parted as she studied the projection. The first thing she noticed was that it was naked! Though how else were you supposed to accurately study anatomy? Even so, it took her a moment to adjust to the sight before her. If it wasn't for the slight glow and the fact Tori knew it had to be a hologram, she would have thought a real person was in the room with them. Not surprisingly, it towered over her. The same size as Aderus, if not bigger. Her gaze flitted between the two, comparing. In fact, there seemed to be very little difference in appearance.

Tori slowly stood, her food all but forgotten, and stepped around the image, her eyes fixing on every detail. The woman's chest was flat and muscular, with a patch of rough, patterned-looking skin that ran from just below each collarbone to the center of her chest. She had the same patterns along her outer forearms, shins and up her spine, but the ridges were more pronounced—like blunt, thick spines. Tori's eyes locked on an elbow and her eyes widened. There was a deadly-looking protrusion that extended from the bone that formed her elbow. It tucked neatly against the back of her arm, almost invisible unless one looked closely. She shuddered at the thought of what it would feel like to be elbowed by one of them. Did Aderus have the same protrusions on his body?

Then she looked down. Four large toes. And not surprisingly, they sported the same black claws as her fingers. What *was* surprising, however, is that the digits formed not a line but a pattern where the middle two toes protruded forward while the first and last hung back, giving it a very different appearance from a human foot. After a few moments of gawking, Tori finally forced her gaze up to her groin. She blinked as she saw roughened patches covered that area, too. She bent her knees a little and squinted—there was no indication of any opening, no outer labia lips. Huh, strange. Yeah. And here *she* was, peering at a non-existent alien woman's private bits.

Tori quickly righted herself and stepped back.

Large ginger eyes blinked down at her, a curled upper lip that revealed too many teeth. A chill ran down Tori's spine. *It's just a hologram.* Only, suddenly, she wasn't so sure. A bone-chilling hiss made her go still, followed by that ominous clicking. The female slowly lowered her head, looking like she was preparing to attack. Tori's eyes widened.

"She is convincing."

Aderus stood directly behind her and she spun to face him. "For Christ's sa—" Her voice breathless.

He took his gaze from the hologram. "It is a virtual display."

"I know. But she *seems so real*." She frowned, her gaze going back to the image that was now in a full-on crouch, swiping viciously at her with claws that looked like they could rend her in two.

Tori stepped closer to Aderus. The thing was freaking her out. Human holograms were not nearly as life-like. "So, her behavior is authentic?"

Aderus didn't answer except to rumble low in the back of his throat. It almost sounded appreciative. And as Tori watched him watching the display, his admiration was obvious, even to her. Part of her felt a small stab of disappointment. She could guess what he saw when he looked at her then, about as appealing as a stick.

"Females are brutal and aggressive," he finally said, eyes still locked on the display. "They are attractive qualities to a male. She looks for a male that can match, or preferably best, her. This ensures strong progeny."

Her brows rose. With the image he painted Tori could only imagine what sex would be like. As her gaze fell back to the snarling, hissing beast before them she pictured it involved her beating the living shit out of a male twice her size and if he wasn't limping away at the end holding his detached balls, then all right, let's fuck? Tori quickly bit her lip as she tried not to laugh. She didn't know why the thought struck her as so funny, but it did. Hell, this saucy little vid was probably their version of porn, she realized, then frowned in annoyance, crossing her arms over her chest.

Her gaze wandered as she tried to ignore the thought. "I haven't seen any aboard the ship." She prodded as she watched for Aderus's reaction. They had made it known there were no females of their kind aboard their vessel—something about the nature of their escape. But there was a lot of rumor-mongering, even among Earth government officials, that it was a ploy. That there were likely females aboard the ship and they were just hiding them away for some reason. Tori had to admit, she wondered how he'd answer.

"We were kept separately and could not free them."

His gaze was averted, and Tori imagined she could hear the anguish in his voice. She felt an answering pang in her chest. "I'm so sorry. That's awful. How long were you imprisoned?"

She watched his fingers twitch. "More than two Earth years. Some much longer."

She swallowed and looked down. The Askari called them *Maekhurz*. Tori couldn't imagine that a species with such little regard for another advanced and intelligent race or their world had treated them very well, so she didn't ask.

"What did you do before you were captured?" she questioned softly.

He stared back at her. "I fought."

"I meant, what was it you did before the fighting? Did you have a profession or...? Particular skill? You've led most of the interactions with Earth governments so far," she gently prodded. "Were you a diplomat of some sort?"

Her last question earned a clipped hiss. "Not a diplomat."

"Okay then."

"We have fought since before I was birthed."

"Oh."

Tori couldn't imagine knowing nothing but fighting your entire life. Not being able to pursue different dreams, a better life. She couldn't help feeling she'd stuck her foot in it.

"Well, maybe now with the alliance, you can choose to pursue something that interests you."

The silence stretched. It seemed the large Askari had discussed all he cared to on the subject.

Chapter Sixteen

Aderus glared across the small gathering, his claws curling painfully into flesh. He had heard talk the past few *sols*, knew of the growing sentiment surrounding the human *khurzha's* attack. His jaw clenched as he listened to yet another speak out *against* allying with Earth.

"We trade for access to their metals, but they are no more than a hindrance fighting alongside us."

It was Krim who countered. "They offer more. We could return with vessels. We could take back *Dravhim*".

A large scarred male called Xaphan spoke next, teeth flashing in a near snarl. "I held hope their females could help us, after what I saw of human *men*. And they allow both to fight."

Jadar, who had been standing silently to his right, responded evenly. "They are aware of their weaknesses, and still offer aid. Let them worry about their own lives."

They stood in the corridor outside of the hold, where a majority were still recovering. A few had healed enough to join the conversation, thanks to the *synth blood* Tori had brought, but it wasn't looking favorable. His fragile optimism was being replaced by anger that the others could not see an opportunity they would not have again. Jadar was right, let the humans worry about their own lives. Physically, they were no match for even *Maekhurz* but Askari technology would help, and if they could take back a large stronghold as *Dravhim,* they could free enough of their own kind and ships that they would no longer need the humans.

His thoughts drifted again to Tori. He knew what they said was true. Her attack on the *palkriv* had shown just how pathetic humans would be in a fight. And the male hadn't even been trying.

Both sides had purely selfish motives, but the Earthers had displayed a surprising tenacity, despite their disadvantages—the small *whitz* of a female had at least demonstrated that much. They were willing to face certain death for a world not their own and a people who viewed them as inferior. A deep hiss, followed by two clicks burst from his throat, effectively silencing the group.

"They are weaker, fragile, so we know. It is their nature. So, you are willing to deny an opportunity, however small, to take *Dravhim*? Save our people, even Askara? Because they are not an ideal or *easy* ally?"

***

Deep breath in. Slooow, easy exhale. Tori sat in her quarters, feeds monitoring each room as she still sported her glittering alien leotard. She was quickly developing an attachment to it, especially considering the past 24 hours.

In a few minutes she'd be escorted to the Askari vessel where, it felt like once again, the fate of the alliance rested solely on her shoulders. And on her ability to prove that humans weren't the pathetic weaklings their extraterrestrial guests thought them to be. Only fitting she be the one to do so, seeing as her impulsive superhero stunt was the reason they were refusing Earth's offer.

Yesterday morning felt like she'd woken to a nightmare when Wells had promptly comm-ed her after a meeting with Aderus and Jadar. In an instant she had half a dozen high-ranking officials jumping down her throat. *"What the hell happened?!" "They view us as a liability." "You lied on an official report, Doctor." "What aren't you telling us?"* One in particular still rang heavy in her ears. *"Either find a way to fix this, or your failed career will be the least of your worries."*

She'd panicked and offered the first thing that came to mind. The simplest solution. If the Askari saw her as an incompetent weakling, prove them wrong. Go on the offense, show she was capable, show she could fight. Unfortunately, the only effective way to do that, to truly sway their opinion, would be to attack and subdue one of their own…

Aderus.

Tori's heart sank for the millionth time at the thought. She had worked hard to gain his trust. They had a bond, she felt. The closest human-Askari association since their races had been introduced mere days before. And it was because of that familiarity that he'd be the only one with whom she had a remote chance of success. By exploiting a budding friendship.

All that was gained, her hope for continued progress, could be lost in mere minutes.

Tori wasn't delusional; she knew even with the grueling training she had received in the past 24 hours she'd still have a slim chance in Hell of "subduing" his ass, let alone causing any significant harm. She'd seen them fight, knew first-hand what they were capable of. The mere thought of attacking one of them was insane. She was depending largely on the element of surprise, their gross underestimation of human ability and lastly, on Aderus's seeming protectiveness toward her, which she had witnessed more than once in their dealings together. She doubted it was anything more than diplomatic necessity on his part, but she was counting on the fact that even once he realized what she was doing he'd act with restraint to avoid truly hurting her. She wasn't sure any of the others would. Even then, she didn't expect him to go easy on her. The impression she'd gotten was that weakness wasn't coddled.

Tori swallowed again, trying to wet her dry throat. Her gaze landed on the fully stocked med bag on the floor near the door. The only good that came out of this psychotic escapade was unlimited access to the stock room, including twelve pints of synth blood. No one had questioned her, considering the high likelihood of serious injury, even death, with what she was about to do.

Self-doubt is your most dangerous opponent.

She heard one of the instructors' mantras repeat in her mind. The two men and woman who worked with her yesterday were the elite—people who killed for a living and didn't exist in a database, she was sure. They had taught her the most basic and effective maneuvers to bring down a bigger opponent and made her repeat them until her bones ached and her body ran on autopilot. That was the goal—master a few moves so well that she could perform them without thinking. So, after twelve hours of unrelenting training yesterday she had awoken this morning with red-rimmed eyes. Despite being the most physically exhausted she'd ever been in her life, Tori hadn't slept well. Big surprise. She knew she was running on pure adrenaline.

Her fingers brushed along a dark sleeve of the *havat*. She knew now it was enhancing her physical abilities. Nothing super-human, but impressive nonetheless. Her instructors had noticed it right away; it made her hits harder, her blocks more effortless; she could jump higher and take a brutal hit that might otherwise have broken bone. Essentially, she was on par with a highly trained operative three times her size. Yep, Henry was most definitely her new best friend. And likely the thing that would save her life. It gave her assurance she sorely needed.

Tori worried her bottom lip. She had to get her nerves under control. If she was fidgety and trembling with her heart pounding out of her chest, they'd know instantly something was up. So, she swallowed hard and went back to breathing to calm herself.

Deep breath in. Slooow, steady exhale.

It couldn't have been more than ten minutes when the door chime went off. She clenched her jaw and rose to meet Wells and one of her instructors from the day before.

"How do you feel?" Wells questioned, his light brown eyes searching for a confidence she didn't feel.

"As well as can be expected," she replied, just wanting to get this over with.

"Do you want to spar a bit more before we go?" The man was huge, rivaling Aderus in height.

"No. I'm as ready as I'm going to be."

Chapter Seventeen

Something was different. Aderus couldn't quite place it, but there was something in the way she carried herself. A prickling sensation along his skin ushered a sense of apprehension. They moved through the vessel, on their way to where the rest were waiting, whether still recovering or not. Tori carried a large *med bag,* laden with supplies, and, she assured, more *synth blood*.

Aderus should be pleased, relieved. Instead he felt an odd sensation of foreboding. An Askari's senses were never wrong. Perhaps one of the others planned something sinister. He looked down at the female, the *havat* he had given her forming to and glimmering against her colorless skin as she struggled slightly to match his strides while toting her burden. Krim led the way and Vepar followed. He had not missed how the latter male stared curiously at her chest and an unexpected feeling of annoyance stole over him. She seemed oblivious to their attentions, however. As a female their own kind would act.

Something was definitely different, he thought, ears flicking in agitation. She hadn't moved to grab at him through the decontamination process. Instead she'd seemed unaffected. Not that he minded; her newly found control was far more appealing. He'd watched her stand silent beside them, waiting calmly for the process to finish, his eyes lingering on her slight frame, now so easily visible. Surprisingly, the covering suited her.

Had he not chosen to trust her, Aderus might be suspicious. It was why they had again refused to allow any but the small *khurzha* aboard when the humans had requested a "meeting" to demonstrate their worthiness as allies. Tori insisted she could convince the others if she could only speak with them.

Aderus admitted, it rekindled his hope. He was extra vigilant in escorting her through the ship but discarded any suspicions the closer they got. It was unlikely her strange behavior should give cause for concern when she had done nothing but help them. And she couldn't possibly be carrying weapons, their technology would have detected them. It didn't even enter his thoughts that she would be a threat physically to any one of them. He was far more focused on the males around them as they entered the hold and she spoke to all that were gathered to hear what would convince them to change their minds regarding the alliance with Earth... Until the little human turned on him mere moments later. Aderus's eyes dilated with disbelief, his mind costing him the precious seconds necessary for her to overtake him.

***

Tori had miraculously managed to keep her nerves in check through sheer strength of will. That Goddess-damned Decon chamber of theirs had nothing on the shit that was about to go down. Her steps almost faltered as she entered the large area where they were keeping their injured and she saw all thirty or so Askari gathered and waiting, some more patiently than others, to hear what she had to say.

Her head tilted back as she stepped past Aderus, taking in the vast ceiling and high walls. The place was huge. There were towering, pulsing columns that framed the walls to either side toward the back of the space and she guessed they might be what powered the ship. She didn't have time to gawk, though, as sixty un-Earthly eyes pinned her with their stares. Some were lying on the strange floating tables, barely able to hold themselves upright. She swallowed once, far from oblivious to the fact that their gazes were roaming over her, consuming in their intensity. She looked to Aderus, but his focus was firmly on those around them. Vepar and Krim were similarly distracted. She briefly caught Jadar's verdant stare and slight incline of his head among the crowd and she returned the gesture with a small smile, the seeming vote of support exactly what she needed. Tori clenched her hands then cleared her throat.

"Hello. Some of you have already met me, but I know many of you haven't. My name is Victoria Davis and I'm the emergency medical specialist aboard one of our most advanced ships, the *Phoenix*. I know you're a species of few words, so I'll try to keep it brief." She hesitated, trying to remember what she wanted to say.

"Before you came, we thought we were alone." Tori paused, letting the weight of that statement find feeling because it was true; micro bacteria were not the same as sentient, humanoid beings.

"You represent a future where humans can be more than a blip on the cosmic timescale, sparked to life only to burn out quickly and be forgotten as if we never existed. Where we can expand our knowledge and our race, experience the universe... Become more than what we are. Hopefully, alongside and as friends to the Askari. That is worth more to us than anything else." Her eyes scanned the crowd as she spoke. "It also goes against our nature to stand by while injustices are committed, and what is being done to you and yours is deplorable. We may not be as strong or as fast as your kind, but that doesn't mean we can't fight, that we wouldn't be advantageous allies. Our race is resilient, resourceful and we can learn quickly."

Tori compressed her lips as she physically and mentally prepared herself for what was to come. A quick look to her right showed that Aderus was a few short feet away, and Krim and Vepar were closer to the others than herself. This was it. She began side-stepping as she spoke, each time moving closer to the large golden-eyed Demon.

"I'm aware that to many of you I'm...freakish, as a female," she said in a low tone. "Our races are different that way. I know that the consequences of my actions a few days ago are what convinced most of you to refuse our offer. But I'm here to demonstrate that being an effective fighter isn't always about size and brute strength."

As the last words left her lips Tori turned toward Aderus. As she had hoped, he was still facing away, his eyes on the others. Her heart spiked, her muscles tensed and the sleeves of her *havat* dropped past her wrists to cover her knuckles (a nifty little response to her body's reactions, which they had learned during training). She moved without thinking, so fast that her mind tripped to keep up with what her body was doing, but then that was the point.

She struck his foot first. Aderus's head turned a scant second before she made contact and Tori watched his large eyes expand in what could only be disbelief as her heel came down hard on an area she guessed might be vulnerable from her study of the hologram the other day. But that wasn't her real target.

Her movements were lightning quick and fluid as she brought her knee up high and hard in almost the same motion.

A growled grunt and something akin to pain transformed his features.

Regret, relief and a surprising satisfaction crashed through her. Regret that she had hurt him, that she was destroying his trust in her. Relief that they had been right in assuming their weaknesses, and yes, a perverse satisfaction that she could prove to him she wasn't some pathetic wisp of nothing that didn't even deserve a second glance, let alone his respect. The dark feeling tore through her and Tori clung to it for strength.

She needed him to bend to reach her next target and the groin blow accomplished that. Time seemed to slow as she watched his beautiful eyes narrow and heavy locks fall forward to cover his ears. In the same heartbeat she struck. She punched his throat as hard as she possibly could, in the exact location her instructors had hammered into her. She heard a sickening crunch. Snarling, hissing shouts registered faintly in the background. And even though she could tell she had really injured him, she couldn't stop. She had to finish it.

With one final push of determination, Tori jumped to haul herself onto his back, as she'd done with the pale-skinned male before. Adrenaline flowed heavy through her veins, powering her muscles, and she held herself there with both arms around Aderus's neck. Her thighs, even stretched wide, couldn't grip his sides, so she clung tight and pulled her legs up, digging her feet into his backside to hold her weight. Tori breathed hard, looking up at a wide-eyed Krim and Vepar. Jadar had pushed himself to the front of the group as the others watched on. She had assumed the noises she'd heard were those of outrage, but while some held the same shocked look as her escorts, as she scanned the crowd, most watched with a different expression. One of seeming rapt fascination and...excitement? The realization was unsettling.

A choking wheeze drew her attention back and regret washed over her in a consuming wave. Tori felt the prick of tears as Aderus struggled to breathe and she readied herself to release her hold on his back. She had proved what she set out to; she had incapacitated him, unarmed, enough to deal a killing blow. But what had she lost in the process?

Thought ceased in the next instant, however, as her world was literally flipped upside down. Clawed fingers enveloped her upper arm and shoulder and before Tori even knew what was happening, she was on her hands and knees gazing at the floor.

Oh shit.

The breath was knocked from her and her knees nearly gave as an impossible weight slammed against her back. It was Aderus. Tori saw dark fingers curl into the metal floor a foot above her head. Her breath finally found her in a great, sucking gasp and settled into a ragged panicked rhythm. *Oh Goddess. Please don't kill me.*

"Ader—" she tried to choke out, but a stirring of her hair preceded an almighty hiss, followed by vicious, clicking growls that sent terror down her spine. She felt what she thought were teeth touch her ear and something inside her reacted, but it was the opposite of what she intended. Instead of staying still, non-threatening, she threw her head back to collide with what must have been his nose. Pain came in a blinding rush—fuck, their skulls were hard—and Tori swayed under the onslaught.

She barely heard the swelling crowd, and as soon as she realized what she'd done she froze.

Tori felt a momentary lift of his weight only to be slammed face first into the floor. She turned her head at the last second to avoid the collision, but her temple still cracked painfully against the metal and she cried out. Her skull throbbed, but she tried hard to push past the pain. A large hand held her pressed to the floor in the center of her back and she was still on her knees. Through the *havat*, she could feel Aderus's claws biting into her flesh. A sob fought its way free of her throat, and she tried to struggle, wanted to go out fighting if this was the end, but her vision darkened as he leaned over her, his dark locks falling forward to shut out the feet and legs of those around them.

Her neck twisted painfully as her eyes rolled back. She winced when he let loose a grated snarl in her face.

"Please," she begged.

Then her breath caught on a hiccup as she felt something against her backside. Something large and hard that couldn't possibly be anything else but him. Her eyes widened. For a moment she thought she might be imagining it, a likely concussion making her delusional. Then she watched as the big Askari realized it as well. The snarling halted abruptly, and his burning eyes took on a different intensity. Tori felt his flesh turn rigid around her and even his breathing ceased.

A handful of seconds ticked by like that, gazes locked in disbelief, neither of them moving a muscle. She wasn't sure how to process what she felt in that moment, let alone what it meant.

Then Tori felt a hard jolt, almost as if something large and heavy had fallen right next to them and in the next instant she was alone on the floor, surrounded by a circle of on-lookers. She collapsed shakily onto her rear. She felt disoriented, overcome by the crowd, by everything that had just happened. Aderus stood looking down at her, his chest heaving, muscles so tight they seemed to tremble. Their audience was eerily silent.

She could feel dozens of gazes boring into her, but her eyes only sought his. The fury of betrayal swirled in them and feeling tore through her.

Her eyes stung as she tried to push herself up. "Aderus," she said, putting every ounce of regret she could into it. "I'm sorry."

But he said nothing, just stared down at her with a look so scorching it was painful.

Then he turned and stormed toward the corridor, leaving her in a shaky mess on the floor in front of over two dozen of his kind. She couldn't let things end like this. She had survived the whole ordeal relatively unharmed, but the emotional consequences were another thing entirely. Tori pulled herself up, stumbling after him. She had to explain, had to make him understand.

Someone, or maybe it was multiple someones, called out in their guttural language and for a moment she expected they were going to stop her but was relieved when she moved forward unobstructed. If any of them followed, she couldn't say, and didn't care. So long as they didn't get in her way.

She caught up with Aderus down the corridor, just as he was turning to walk through another one of those door-barrier things, and panicked. She was damn sure she'd be unable to follow so she threw herself the last few feet and latched on to his arm just as he slipped through the barrier.

He threw her off of him into the room and Tori stumbled several times to regain her footing, turning to face the enraged being before her.

"You *dare*!!" he hissed, bearing down on her, double rows of sharp teeth clearly on display. "*You do not know what you have done!*"

She flinched and took several steps back. His two-toned voice rasped, and she knew it was from the blow she'd dealt him. They healed quickly, but concern momentarily punched her gut. It was swiftly overcome by terror. She knew she deserved whatever he had to dish out, but facing his unleashed fury was frightening as fuck. And there were no others around, they were alone in this room. Warning bells blared in Tori's head. What had she been thinking, running after him like that?

He advanced to tower over her and by some miracle Tori held her ground. She jumped when he reached out to grip her jaw in one large hand. It was the first time he had initiated a touch and the circumstances weren't lost on her. His palm encircled her throat and dread seized her at the feel of sharp claws in her hair. A whimpering sound escaped from the back of her throat.

He leaned down, letting loose a fierce clicking growl.

"You *had no right*!" he hissed, and she blinked, fear suddenly replaced by understanding. Not only had she abused his trust, she had humiliated him in front of the others by forcing him to pick between letting her best him or potentially injuring an ambassador of Earth and ending any hope of an alliance that might save their world.

Tori hadn't known the Askari long, but it was obvious they were a prideful people. She'd been obsessing about protecting her own ass, proving humans were a worthy ally, fixing her fuck-up. But she hadn't fully thought things through from his perspective.

Goddess, it made her feel even worse.

Tori swallowed dryly before forcing an answer past her lips. "I know. I know I didn't. But it was the only way I could think of. I didn't *want* to hurt you, use you. Or our friendship," she pleaded, searching for the words to make him understand. His grip on her jaw didn't lessen. "I felt...you were the only one I could trust."

Wrong thing to say.

"*Trust!* You do not understand the meaning of the word!" he roared.

Gaia, he was a sight to behold when angry, his otherworldly features exuding an intensity that was almost beautiful. Tori pulled back at his outburst, but his grip held her immobile, so she reached up to clasp his wrist, which seemed to momentarily distract him. His eyes locked on her hand then lifted back to her face. He seemed to calm a fraction. But then his lip curled, revealing his teeth, and anger quickly returned to his gaze.

"A *real* female could throw me across this room," he growled low and throatily.

Tori blinked at the insult, momentarily stunned. It hit a chord, and the words were past her lips before she could stop them.

"I'm female enough," she voiced in quiet challenge, waiting to see if he would catch the implication. Her mind still whirled over what had happened mere minutes before. She wanted to know.

It took a moment for what she'd said to hit home, but when it did Aderus jerked back as if she'd struck him; his nostrils flared, and he released her almost as quickly as he'd grabbed her.

Tori watched his golden gaze flick back and forth, avoiding her eyes, in obvious discomfort. She felt her cheeks flush. Was the thought *that* repulsive to him? Whatever, it wasn't important. That's not what she was here for.

Aderus straightened and moved back, staring down at her almost warily before his features blanked.

"I will take you back to your ship," he growled. Then his eyes blazed, betraying him. "You can tell your superiors your actions have likely succeeded."

Chapter Eighteen

The days that followed were rough. It seemed her attack on Aderus had worked; the Askari had agreed to a tentative alliance. Earth governments couldn't be happier. Tori wished she could celebrate the achievement, but for her, the costs were personal.

There were no longer any threats to her job. On the contrary, Wells and the others deemed her a most valuable asset and she had since been appointed "Chief Diplomatic Advisor" to the Askari. She was allowed aboard their vessel almost daily, to continue to "help with their injured" (aka provide any needed synth blood), but mainly to start acclimating the large aliens to working with and around humans. There were plans to begin constructing hybrid Earth-Askara battle vessels immediately and both races would need to become comfortable working, living and interacting with one another. The *Amendment* was undergoing major renovations as the Askari had agreed to cohabitate parts of the vessel (specifically, the floor that housed the main docking gate to their ship) in order to facilitate relations.

Tori definitely noticed a difference in the way the other Askari treated her now. It was a confusing mix. Most eyed her warily but with a degree of what she liked to think was respect. Some seemed curious and she would catch them watching her with detached interest. Then there were a small few that acted outright obnoxious. Those were the ones that scared her. They seemed violent, unstable—hissing and snapping, though it was never aimed at her directly. It was always deflected onto another Askari and Tori couldn't figure out what she was doing to agitate them, other than the fact they just didn't care for humans. She wasn't naïve and didn't expect all individuals were going to be accepting toward her. Just as she knew not all people were going to be accepting toward their extraterrestrial allies. Though, with any hope, the grueling interview process and background checks put into place recently would mostly stem that problem from Earth's side.

Tori had tried more than once to talk to Aderus in the days since their confrontation, but it seemed their relationship was damaged beyond repair. He still escorted her whenever aboard their vessel, but things were definitely not the same. He hardly looked at her and only spoke to her when absolutely necessary. Most of the time he let one of the others answer questions she directed at him. After a while, Tori stopped trying.

Days that should be filled with wonder and excitement were weighted down by her own guilt, and Tori couldn't hide the fact it was making her miserable. She wasn't a naturally violent person and the actions of their encounter had not come easily to her. Nor, it seemed, did dealing with the consequences. She could only hope that things would blow over in time. But that didn't really help her right now.

Liv knew something was up and though she couldn't know the details of the situation, her vid calls lately usually consisted of her best friend threatening she'd somehow get access to come aboard, if only to make sure she was taking care of herself. Tori couldn't deny sleep was harder to come by lately and the stress was taking its toll. She felt like shit.

So, she shouldn't have been surprised at her lack of restraint when tensions finally came to a head.

***

It was several *sols* after the humiliating display with the *khurzha* and he was still struggling with his emotions. He was angry with the female. He resented her deceit and knew now he could not trust her. But if he were honest, Aderus directed most of the rage at himself. He was furious that he had not listened to his senses, frustrated that it had led to him having to let her best him in front of the others or else risk killing or severely injuring an Earth diplomat, which would have cost them the alliance, if not their lives.

A logical part of him understood why she had deceived him and even acknowledged a difficult but necessary decision, but he didn't want to listen to that part. It was far more appealing to let resentment rule. Especially because hiding beneath it all was disbelief and confusion. Yes, he was not juvenile enough to discount those were the real emotions driving him.

The disgrace of such a weak being getting the better of him in front of a room full of battle-hardened Askari was a big part of his anger. Even bigger, however, was the way in which his body had involuntarily reacted to her attack. It had shocked and horrified him. His *pvost* had hardened as if it sought to breed her. A frail alien no bigger and with less strength than a youngling! There was something wrong with him.

It had simply been too long since his last breeding...so long, he couldn't exactly remember. Even as he reasoned it was so, an image of the pale-skinned human came to mind and he had to admit to some small measure of appreciation. He had let her best him, but her speed and strength had surprised him. It appeared the *havat* enhanced a human's abilities to a much greater extent that it did an Askari, a puzzling and pertinent fact they would have to explore in more depth. Though, he supposed it only strengthened their potential worthiness as allies.

Her show of aggression was what likely triggered his baser instincts, Aderus assured himself, yet again. One could also not discount their similarities. He'd even go so far as to say there may be some allure to their more elegant forms. But it was how one might appreciate the sight of *Kharhisshna* rising over the jagged peaks of Askara at night, or the vision of a newly formed nebula...

So, Aderus had mostly kept his distance. Not only because he still struggled with his feelings but also to avoid any more mixed signals that would trigger another embarrassing reaction. He could tell his neglect upset her, but perhaps she should have thought of such things before she used him as a demonstration. He didn't let any of it get in the way of his duties, however, which he still took very seriously. He had vowed her safety aboard their vessel and words spoken were not something any Askari took lightly.

His lip curled in annoyance. Especially since some of the males had begun posturing around her. Apparently, it mattered not to them what she was, only that she carried the designation *female*. He was sure the displays were not serious, just responses based on instinct or perhaps boredom. Either way, he was overly vigilant while escorting her with others present and made sure he never strayed far from her side. An overwhelming satisfaction filled him at the fact that they had already started building the vessels that would take back their world. The last thing they needed was for her to get injured as a result of pointless posturing between idiots.

Chapter Nineteen

Tori stifled another yawn as she stood next to Jadar while he monitored a male called Braxas, who had been unconscious since their arrival. The enormous Askari's skin was on the darker side, which was saying something, and he was actually bald with random protrusions along his scalp, like someone had butchered his locks. It was his eyes that made her uneasy, however. They were pure black, the entire orb, with touches of violet. His lids were shut right now, thank Gaia. It was only when Jadar occasionally raised them to check for some type of response that Tori caught a glimpse.

The other thing that was strange were his limbs. His joints were more prominent than the others. It was almost as if he suffered from some type of debilitating disease and she wondered if it affected his mobility at all.

When she found out from Jadar that he had been tortured, her heart broke. Perhaps that explained his different appearance. A blast from the enemy ship had knocked him unconscious during escape and they had been checking him daily but, so far, no change. When she pressed about his eyes, Jadar hadn't answered and she couldn't help but wonder what else had been done to him.

Tori looked around, spotting Aderus several feet away. He guarded her like a mute watchdog when moving about their vessel, but whenever she rounded with Jadar he couldn't get away fast enough. She sighed; his relief was practically palpable. Tori wanted to complain that his refusal to speak to her could compromise her safety, but she refused to take that route.

Movement from the table drew her attention back. Jadar was interacting with a wall display on the other side so he didn't see Braxas's claw twitch on the finger closest her. She looked to his face, watching carefully for any sign the male was waking. His eyelids fluttered; Tori anxiously alerted Jadar.

When she looked back, he was blinking at her with confused, dappled eyes. "Hi there." She was careful to keep her expression blank and spoke slowly. "My name is Tori. Do you know where you are?" The next few moments happened so quickly Tori barely had time to process them.

His heavy-lidded gaze trailed briefly over her person, then his nostrils flared. Black eyes widened, and his expression morphed into something ugly as he lashed out with a snarled hiss. Tori gasped and stumbled back, managing to avoid his sharp claws, but she couldn't dodge the kick he aimed at her hip.

She was vaguely aware of shouting from Jadar as she found herself, once again, propelled through space. The floor came fast and hard but didn't feel as jarring as before and she realized Henry must have absorbed most of the impact. Tori stayed sprawled on the floor for a moment—it and she were good friends by now—trying to catch her bearings as she watched Jadar and two others rush to restrain Braxas. He thrashed violently on the table, black speckled eyes locked on her, and the chilling look he gave her halted the breath in her chest.

It was obvious her presence was enraging him, though she had no idea why. Jadar bellowed when a heavy arm broke free and almost knocked the Healer back as well. It sent her into a near panic and she scrambled to push herself up.

A dark hand suddenly hauled her to her feet as if she weighed nothing. Aderus's unique scent hit her nose. He pushed her away, putting his body between her and the exam table as he hissed something at the others. Relief washed over her. Tori quickly peeked around his side to glimpse Jadar apparently sedating Braxas. Her heart pounded as she watched the huge form go limp.

Then she turned on Aderus, fear still flooding her veins and sparking her temper.

"Are you done punishing me yet? Because I sure as shit am done with the childish behavior. I don't want your help if you can't even be bothered to speak to me." She watched his ethereal eyes broaden at her words, then his lip curled. She was too sleep-deprived and worn down, however, from dealing with him, *not* dealing with her, to heed the warning.

"And *don't* snarl at me!" she growled.

***

Aderus watched her walk away. He was vaguely aware of multiple other eyes that had witnessed yet another display between him and the Earther. Was demeaning him in front of them all before not enough for her? How dare she condemn him, after what she had put him through!

He had protected her, more than once—something he *never* would have had to do for an Askari female—and still she challenged him.

What right did she have to be angry with *him*? None. If the little *khurzha* thought to bend him to her will, she had better think again. A healthy show of strength always afforded respect, he reminded himself. At least that's the way it was with his kind. She clearly did not respect him because she no longer feared him. Perhaps he should remind her.

***

Tori hadn't made it far and was already regretting going off on Aderus. Well, kind of. Part of her felt he deserved it for acting like a vindictive teenager the last week, but the more rational part of her knew she couldn't hold it entirely against him. Considering what she had put him through, he was entitled to some retribution. Even by human standards.

She still felt guilty, too, but was tired of beating herself up about it. What was done was done.

The person back there had not been her, though, and that's what she felt bad about. She was not angry, unstable and disparaging. Just stressed and sleep-deprived. Neither was she used to feeling dependent and not in control. She sighed and slowed her steps. It mattered to her that Aderus understand that.

An odd sensation made her frown and look down. The soft hum of the metal floor had grown rougher, shaky. Then she recognized a rhythm and twisted just in time to see a large body coming at her.

The lethal way Aderus moved halted any words in her throat and Tori immediately tensed. At least she thought it was him. The huge alien had her stumbling back against the hard wall of the corridor so fast she barely had time to process it. A deep hiss followed by four short clicks told her he meant business and she tipped her head back to lock with eyes so penetrating they almost glowed.

"You will not shame me again in front of the others," he rumbled, breath stirring her hair as he spoke.

Tori breathed deep. "You're right. I shouldn't have reacted like that. I'm sorry." She had dropped her eyes to his chest in submission but lifted her gaze now to show her sincerity. "You've looked out for me from the beginning and it was insensitive and ungrateful of me."

He blinked, her words seeming to surprise him. The tension in his long, muscled limbs eased only slightly. Until she gathered her courage and dropped the other shoe.

"But I'm not sorry for what I said."

Something dangerous flickered in his eyes as he loomed over her. Tori kept her hands flat on the wall at her sides. She could feel the heat radiating from his skin.

"You lecture me on behavior?" he hissed softly.

Tori swallowed. She knew what he was getting at. "I already apologized for that, Aderus, and explained the reasons. I can't change what was done. I can only offer a path forward. I hope, in time, you can learn to trust me again. If there was something I could do to fix things between us, I would. But not talking to me isn't the answer." She exhaled a shaky breath. "It makes things needlessly difficult. And dangerous."

His eyes narrowed. "I answer your questions. Talking is useless."

"I beg to differ," she said softly, hoping she wasn't pushing him too far. "We need to be able to communicate and you need to stop avoiding me like the plague. Not that it's not warranted; we just can't afford it. Do you understand?"

Tori watched a muscle in his jaw tick. He wasn't stupid. But he also didn't look ready to move on.

"You should understand that we do not easily trust. Or forgive."

"All I can ask is that you let me try."

Tori searched his eyes, her mood lightening for the first time in days. Perhaps the stoic Askari would let her work her way back into his good graces. He seemed to be struggling with the concept, though, and still held her captive against the corridor wall. The hardness hadn't left his eyes. She knew now it was their way of handling conflict—a show of force until one of them submitted. The tactic had worked on her before because, well, they were intimidating as all get out when they wanted to be. But now that she knew it, Tori held his gaze until he eventually stepped back. His chin lifted, and he stared down at her.

"Thank you for giving me another chance," she said softly and meant it. The faint smile that found its way to her lips felt like a new beginning.

Chapter Twenty

Her relationship with Aderus was slowly on the mend. At least, he was speaking to her again. She sensed a definite guardedness, but that was to be expected, she assured herself. Regaining a broken trust took longer than gaining it in the first place. But she was hopeful and determined. Tori could once again focus on the experiences each day brought with excitement and enthusiasm. She found herself falling into a somewhat easy rapport, at least it felt that way for her. And more and more she failed to see them as aliens and just saw them as people.

She was finally able to follow up on the pale-skinned, crimson-eyed male. He was being monitored in his quarters but was not confined to them. The thought made her uneasy, but apparently it had been that way since the "dispute" between him and Aderus, and in the weeks since she had not seen any sign of him on her daily visits. Tori tried to push for more information but was only told that he had made a full recovery. Despite the fact their last encounter had been frightening (and nearly fatal on her part) she still had an urge to reach out to him. Even stranger, when she asked his name, Jadar had replied he did not know. How could he not know? Had no one tried to talk to him? Did the guy not speak? It seemed very odd.

On the other hand, the large unconscious male that had awoken pissed to high Hell, whom Aderus said they had chosen to name Braxas, had a *severe* aversion to anything alien. Hence his reaction upon waking. Tori had a strong sense that whatever made him feel such extreme hatred had to have something to do with his torture. At any rate, she scarcely saw that one either. He seemed to go out of his way to avoid her, and other than a few disdainful glances from afar on the rare occasion she happened to spot him, one wouldn't even know he was there.

She worked closely with Jadar most days and met more Askari as they all seemingly recovered—thanks to two more hauls of synth blood she'd managed to smuggle aboard. It was a secret she agonized over more and more as time went on. She dreaded the political and media shit storm that would no doubt ensue. Right now, though, she was just trying to focus on learning as much as possible and building good relationships with as many of them as she could.

Jadar seemed the easiest to get on with. The green-eyed healer moved in that fluid, predatory way inherent to their race and there was no denying the intelligence behind those sharp, calculating eyes, but he appeared more subdued than the others. Not that she would ever use the word "gentle" to describe them, but there was a caring way about him.

The vibes she got from Aderus were mixed. Her feelings toward him hadn't faded, which kind of worried her. Tori did her best to ignore them and focus on her job. Each day she woke early and met him at the airlock. She had tried to touch base with Liv as often as possible in the past weeks, but her days were busy. She worked herself until she was asleep on her feet and loved it. Meanwhile, she had taken up residence in one of the new quarters near the docking gate. The rooms were beautiful and spacious, and she loved the two- minute walk to the gate. Getting any of the Askari to move into them, however, had been nearly impossible so far. These things took time, but Wells and his superiors were disappointed and had been pushing her to make progress. With that thought in mind, Tori had invited Aderus to lunch in her quarters, hoping to start a conversation, spark some interest. His refusal had hurt more than she anticipated. But her spirits picked up the next day when he entered the room while she was breaking to eat.

Chapter Twenty-One

Aderus savored the way Tori's face paled as he bit into another *rukhhal*...

The last few *sols* had been a test. Warring was blissfully simple in comparison as he struggled with their new reality. Relations with the humans were progressing slowly, mainly because many Askari in their group were still trying to feel out one another, and that took priority. The others had almost fully recovered, and some were having a harder time coping. All seemed to accept their circumstances, however, and knew an agreement with the Earthers was the best possible option. Even those who were most reluctant perked at the news that construction on Earth-Askara war vessels had already begun.

Wariness and distrust colored their moods, but for many, it was mixed with curiosity, which was encouraging. Aderus had come to know Jadar, Krim and Vepar well enough in their dealings together. He trusted Jadar the most and even considered him friend. The even-tempered healer had been a gift from *Kharhisshna*, something Aderus valued in these tense, unfamiliar times. Earth officials were growing impatient, he knew. But diplomacy was not something Askari excelled at, even among themselves.

The most pressure right now was in letting other humans aboard their vessel. Aderus chafed at the idea, as did others. They would prefer to keep the upper hand and it would put them at a disadvantage. Just the thought kept him awake. But the human ambassador had made clear that if they did not "accommodate" the request soon there would be repercussions.

Earth would withdraw its offer of aid and they would be back where they started.

Aderus clicked his claws in frustration.

He also knew the humans were not happy not a single Askari was interested in quartering on their ship. Were they daft? Of course, no able-minded warrior would willingly put themselves in so vulnerable a position. Not to mention, uncomfortable. Any of them quartering with humans would be gawked at and pestered relentlessly. The Earthlings had yet to grasp they were not "social" in the way humans were. They worked together for common cause, but their social structures existed out of necessity. They did not often agree, fighting was common, and they did not have family units as Earthlings did. Indeed, Aderus could barely remember his *grrhlyen*, as she had set him out at an early age, and few Askari ever met their sires. Theirs was a strictly solitary life.

Eons ago, before his people had learned to harness the abilities of the unique metal of their planet, Askari society had been closer to that of Earth. Perhaps not to the same extreme, but they had been forced to rely on one another more. Co-operate, form lasting associations. But the self-sustaining, self-replicating abilities of their technology had led them to turn inward. In fact, the most unified he could ever remember his people being, was in their fight against the *Maekhurz*. Even the far-removed moon colonies had joined to save their home world. Realizing it gave Aderus an unexpected feeling of pride. If his staunchly independent people could do such things to save themselves, then surely, they could work with the humans?

He realized grudgingly that it would most likely fall on him to appease their demands. And yesterday, as if she had guessed his thoughts, Tori had invited him to meal with her in her quarters. The thought made him extremely uncomfortable, in more ways than one. But he was beginning to accept his fate and the role he was obliged to play if they wanted to continue their dealings with Earth.

He hadn't forgotten how she betrayed him or her second attempt to cow him in front of the others. He still struggled with it, in fact. It wasn't the Askari way to "forgive and forget," as Earthers said. Instead, he chose to focus on what was important and tried to think of all the ways she had helped them since their arrival. He also unwillingly admired her audacity. But every time he allowed himself to feel appreciation, it was followed by an inexplicable surge of anger for what she had done to him personally. Aderus wasn't fool enough to ignore that Tori was the one human they did not want to push away, for all that she had done and could continue to do to help them. Her intentions still seemed genuine. Even her attack on him had, in her mind, been justified. Perhaps if he forced himself to associate with her more his anger would fade, so he had sought her out at midday, remembering how she had reacted with disgust to the nutritious *rukhhal*. It was infantile, but he couldn't help wanting to punish her in some small way. He had purposely chosen an even larger species and was taking his time savoring each wriggling bite. He took a moment to swipe at some innards that coated one finger when he bit into a particularly juicy morsel.

"You're enjoying this, aren't you?" she asked shakily, her strange eyes wide and trained on his meal.

Aderus looked at the bright red cylinder that held some kind of liquid called *soup* where it lay in her lap.

Her look of horror made his snout twitch in delight as she swallowed repeatedly. He held a half-eaten *rukhhal* between his fingers, all the while putting extra emphasis on the pop and crunch of his chews. Something else he remembered she disliked.

She made a breathy noise. "The day I eat that is the day you agree to try a trail bar," she said with a scowl, and Aderus saw a look of challenge flash in her Earthy gaze. His irises narrowed. He was usually very covetous of food, most Askari were, but found himself unable to refuse her dare. He held out a piece, skewered on one of his claws.

Her eyes went wide. "Uhm."

His gaze locked with hers, waiting for her to submit. The thought filled him with triumph, instincts demanding her surrender in any small way to appease him. His excitement faded when her lips tightened and she sat a little straighter. "All right. But that piece is too big."

He rumbled and pulled back to cut a slice with the tip of his claw. She snatched at it quickly, almost as if she doubted her own resolve. But as soon as her fingers came into contact it dropped from her grasp with a high sharp yell. Aderus hissed in annoyance at the almost painful sound. She had dropped it on purpose, he realized, and then jumped back, shaking her hand in apparent revulsion.

"OhmyGods, it's sticky! And it moved!" she almost shrieked. "That's *disgusting*." Again, her high-pitched yells hurt his ears, but his snout now wrinkled and low trills of amusement burst forth from his throat. It felt good. He couldn't remember the last time he had cause for such mirth.

Aderus quickly picked the morsel from the floor and threw it into his mouth. When he looked up her disgust was still apparent. She watched him silently for a moment, tucked back against her seat.

"You're laughing at me." She said, a small smile on her lips.

The quiet words stopped the sound in his throat and he grew guarded, a part of him automatically raising his defenses. It alarmed him that she seemed to have so much influence over him. She shouldn't. He went back to eating.

"Well, hate to disappoint you, but I don't give up that easily."

His eyes flicked up to watch as she again sat a little straighter and leaned forward.

"One more try?" She held up a finger and seemed to plead with him. He huffed and held out a second piece to her in challenge.

She reached out slowly. His jaw ticked. He shoved it toward her. Tori blinked, her eyes flying to his in surprise. And something else he couldn't decipher. She watched him carefully. *Great Kharhisshna, he was running out of patience!* He shoved the piece closer. She would barely have to touch it now.

And then she did something he never expected. The female leaned forward, latched on to his hand with her fingers and plucked the slice from him *with her teeth*. It was as if time stopped. He felt her touch, the warm rush of her breath against his skin, a trace of something soft and wet against his sensitive claw and it shocked him so much he jumped from his seat.

Aderus couldn't even appreciate her reaction—the prompt gagging and choking that ensued as she tried to force the morsel down. Fluid leaked from her eyes, she pounded on her chest and expressions he'd never seen contorted her face. But all he could focus on was what she had done.

Shock faded to be replaced by a range of emotions he couldn't process. Why had she done that? Why?

"Oh Gaia, that was freaking *awful*," Tori coughed. "I think I can still feel the damn thing moving." Aderus watched her fumble with her red cylinder and gulp down some of the contents. But his eyes kept going back to the place her mouth had touched him.

He wanted to feel unaffected but didn't. Instead he felt...affronted? Unsettled? Intrigued?

"Why did you do that?" he demanded, eyes blazing down at the pale-skinned human.

"What?" she asked distractedly, still trying to compose herself.

"Why did you touch me with your mouth?"

At that her head shot up. Shining blue and white eyes widened with...surprise? She had been the one to touch him!

At first her color paled, then the skin of her face and neck bloomed a brilliant red. She was uncomfortable. She should be, he thought. She had no right to touch him that way.

"Oh my Gods, I'm sorry, I thought you were offering," she spoke hurriedly. "It just grossed me out so much the first time and I thought if I could grab it quick with my teeth..." She trailed off. "I guess, I assumed—" One hand touched her forehead. "I don't know what I was thinking."

He growled back, surprised by his own vehemence. "Our claws are sensitive."

"Oh! I hurt you?" She immediately stood. "I'm so sorry."

She hadn't hurt him at all, but he didn't feel like giving her that consolation. He felt strange. Almost frantic. His breathing picked up. He didn't like how he felt.

She stepped toward him. "That was inappropriate and I'm sorry if I offended you, but it truly wasn't meant that way. I'm honestly surprised I was comfortable enough to have even acted on the impulse." She appeared shocked at her own behavior but took a hesitant step closer. "I feel horrible, let me see." When he realized she intended to grab his hand he jerked away with a hiss and bared his teeth.

"*Oh,*" she gasped and grabbed at her hand. He saw pain in her expression but only when the scent of blood hit his nose did he realize he must have caught her with his claws. His nostrils flared, greedily taking it in.

He needed away from her. *Now.*

***

Aderus seemed unhinged and Tori's stomach dropped at the thought she'd hurt him. Though, it couldn't have been *that* bad. She'd seen them fight, claws flying, and she'd barely touched him! The thought made her frown in confusion as she tried to figure out what was really going on.

She'd seen him angry and vicious; this wasn't that. Instead, he looked...almost panicked. She blinked and kept her eyes trained on his agitated movements.

"Just take a deep breath and tell me what's wrong."

She wanted him to talk to her and tried again to step closer, raising her hand in a soothing gesture. She didn't mean to grab him, but maybe he took it that way, because dark fingers locked on to her wrist almost painfully in the next instant and swung her backward. Tori gasped, trying to find her footing and collided with a chair—they moved so damn fast. A low clicking growl sounded above her. He held her hand high over her head and away from him and Tori swallowed. Her eyes were level with his chest and it was apparent he was really worked up. She reached behind her and braced her other hand on the seat back. The cut from his claws stung, but it wasn't bleeding much, just a scratch.

"Aderus? Talk to me." She didn't try to meet his gaze, just kept her eyes looking straight ahead.

"You should not have done that," he said again, in tones equally grating and guttural.

"Yes, and I apologized. I wasn't trying to touch you just now, so can you please let me go?" she replied. He loomed over her as he'd done in the corridor and Tori struggled for understanding. This might be normal behavior between Askari, but it was not going to fly with other people, *when* they finally allowed them aboard.

"Enough. Let go," she said firmly and bucked, pushing him. To her surprise, he released her immediately. But that wasn't what shocked her. She'd felt something... Her eyes flared in recognition. Tori looked up and caught a glimpse of wild, almost fearful, eyes and her lips parted as she struggled to find what to say. It didn't matter, however, because in the next instant, she was staring at a retreating back.

So, that was it? He was just going to run away?

"Coward." The word had flown from her mouth before she could stop it.

He froze and puffed up, body going rigid. If weakness and fear were loathsome, then she'd just issued the ultimate insult.

He didn't face her but growled lowly. "What do you say to me?"

"You heard me," she countered. "If you were human, you'd be acting like one. Running away instead of facing something that—" Tori halted. Did she really have the courage to say it? Her heart raced. Part of her was jumping up, waving a big "STOP!" sign.

"Aderus, I think I'm...attracted. To you." There! She'd said it!

It was almost painful as she waited to see how he'd react.

His broad back was still to her and the only noise was the subtle hum of the ship. Tori started to sweat. Maybe she shouldn't have done that. Maybe she didn't know shit. But what else could it have been? At the very least, calling him out would reveal the truth. Even if it meant exposing her own vulnerability. She cleared her throat.

"I was shocked, too, at first. I mean, you're very different from—never mind," she rambled nervously. "Point is, I think that you...that there might be, you could feel the same. And it's okay. What happened in the cargo hold, if you're at all similar to human men then—"

Aderus was practically on top of her in the next instant. His golden eyes swimming as they flicked over her face and body and his locks puffed out, making him appear even bigger.

"You think a creature such as you could interest me in that way?" he spat lowly, second row of sharp teeth flashing.

Tori jerked back. No one had ever spoken to her so nastily and the words hit her as brutally as any blow, but the hurt was replaced quickly by rage. A loud crack sounded through the room. She had never slapped anyone in her life, but she'd hit him so hard her hand was numb.

Shock registered on both their faces before Aderus snarled and whipped her about, clicking and hissing in her ear.

Tori should be afraid, but his behavior only fueled her rage. This was how they settled a *dispute*, huh? She reached up blindly, latching on to his braids. He hissed viciously as she twisted, and it brought them both to their knees. Aderus retaliated by grabbing her ponytail and yanking to the opposite side. Tori gasped and gritted her teeth. Okay, that didn't feel so good. His claws dug into her scalp even as she knew he was holding back. He could easily crush her skull if he wanted. The knowledge just pissed her off more and she struggled against him.

"Desist," he growled, the word barely understandable.

"Screw you," Tori gritted.

"Submit," he pushed, panting. She was panting, too. She still had a grip on his hair that she was sure felt none too good for him.

"Never," she growled back. Now that she knew how he saw her, Tori refused to back down, even in the face of impossibility. Her pride demanded it. But there was a niggling at the back of her mind, like her brain was trying to tell her something. And then she felt it. The hardness again, against her lower back.

Tori stopped struggling. She loosened her grip and swallowed. She felt the exact moment he realized it, too, because his hold lessened, and he stilled. It was like a repeat of before. Except she wouldn't be the one to state the obvious. She waited for him to say something, do something. But when a full minute passed with nothing but their tense bodies and labored breaths, Tori gave up. All the fight left her.

"Let me up," she demanded, sounding tired and defeated. What was she doing? She didn't know what the hell had come over her. The big Askari just seemed to get to her; he brought out a side of her that was violent and unsettling. Why had she let it happen? Why did she even push him on something that was totally inappropriate and pointless?

She hadn't realized he still held her hair until she felt the glide of his claws against her scalp as he released her. When his weight eased, she pushed herself up and this time it was she who walked away. She stopped at the door and spoke over her shoulder.

"You have my word, this won't be an issue from here on out." Then she left.

Chapter Twenty-Two

Aderus couldn't stop thinking about it. She wanted to breed him?

Several *sols* after the Earth female's confession and what had initially mortified him now consumed his waking thoughts. She had guessed what the reactions of his body meant, forced him to confront them. It had made him react and he had attacked her in a human way, with words.

Such things felt forbidden, strange. But she appeared to accept it easily. Aderus even admired her candor. Askari were fearless when it came to physical risk, but emotions were a different thing.

What about him attracted her, he wondered.

He had been, and still was, struggling with his feelings. But her response to his rejection had changed something within him, once he had allowed himself to explore it. The *khurzha* had no control over her appearance, her small size or the fact she wasn't Askari, but he had witnessed a ferocity, one she kept hidden. Every time he glimpsed it, his body responded. He realized, the things she'd done that made him feel ill toward her would have been flattering coming from an Askari female. But his mind and pride had prevented him from seeing it. He had fought his instincts hard, though they were never wrong.

Once he accepted the truth, apprehension colored his moods. On Askara, a female readily rejected a male if he did not prove himself worthy, but males rarely rejected a female. Perhaps if she were sickly or deranged, but Tori was, he felt, superior among her kind. She had risked much to help them, still did. She was bold and determined in her dealings with them, where other humans were not. Her appearance was...different. But not as off-putting to him now as it once was. Even her odd color of pale, which was not a desirable trait, did not deter him.

He knew enough about human anatomy to understand Earthers birthed young, which meant they reproduced internally as well. It was strange to entertain those ideas, but if she was drawn to him then she had done so as well, he was sure. And he was curious. As the only one of their group who had managed to attract female interest, no matter that she was alien, he would be open to her attentions, he decided. Unless...he was not the only one? The thought soured his mood more than he'd have thought possible and he subsequently caught himself posturing against Krim or Vepar more than once around her. Though, if anything, it seemed to push her away. Usually to seek out Jadar to "round on patients."

Aderus grew frustrated. He did not know what he had done to gain her interest in the first place and noticed she treated him differently now. She was distant, disengaged. It was normal female behavior, but somehow, he'd grown to expect her endless questions. Especially now he knew she saw him as more than just a curiosity.

Pestering from the Ambassador had only increased as well. It seemed the diplomat hounded him daily to discuss "integration of living quarters" and letting skilled humans aboard their vessel to help with repairs. Today was no exception.

"...I think you'll be impressed, once you see what we're talking about. The new wing is truly extraordinary. And it would go a very long way to satisfying my superiors. Which, I assure you, would only be helping yourselves," Wells added in a low tone and what Aderus now believed to be fake enthusiasm.

He stared down the Ambassador, who clasped his hands expectantly at his lack of response. He was tired of this conversation. Was his answer supposed to change the more they asked the same question? The male had caught him at the gate between their two vessels.

"Whomever is interested could come aboard for a meal. Dr. Davis and I would be happy to show you around."

Aderus straightened, his nostrils flaring with intent. "I will gather those who are interested. We will come."

"Of course. I understand," the diplomat began in a placating tone. "You certainly—you will?! That's—excellent, just excellent." He grinned, his excitement appearing genuine.

"The *khurzha* knows of our dietary needs," he interrupted before the male began blathering.

"I-I'm sorry?" Wells stuttered.

"Tori."

"Ohh. Yes, of course," he said, frown clearing. "I'll be sure to consult with her immediately."

Aderus realized then that the *doctor* had learned much about his kind in the time he'd known her, but he knew little of humans in comparison. And the more he thought on it, the more apparent how dangerously unwise it was that they did not know more. In war, one should strive to know thy enemy, but he was learning it was the same with peacekeeping. It wasn't just about false familiarity and obligatory inanities. The risk was greater in what they did not know, in keeping themselves detached.

He had also been waiting for Tori to approach him again. It was what a female Askari would have done. But he was starting to see the problem; he was comparing her to an Askari when she was not one.

Chapter Twenty-Three

Tori rubbed the sleeve of her *havat* for probably the fifth time in ten minutes. Henry pulsed softly back at her. She was not nervous. Surprised maybe. Curious. Excited. But not nervous, no.

How Wells had convinced them to come to the new wing, she had no idea. But why did she have to accept when they volunteered *her* quarters? Her suite was adjacent to the model, which connected with the arboretum. It was a spectacular greenhouse—greenpalace, more like—that contained some of the largest and most beautiful plants from Earth; ideal living quarters for someone higher up, like a diplomat, for instance. Which, she had to remind herself again, she was now.

Stop being a baby, Victoria. If he *wasn't coming, you'd be over the moon about it.* Again, she wished she'd never opened her stupid mouth to Aderus about how she felt. It wasn't personal, she reminded herself.

Right. So much for honesty.

She'd practically mastered the whole cold, professional vibe since then. Not that he seemed to notice. A few times she'd come close to slipping back to her old self. Tori didn't like playing the part of ice-cold bitch. It was exhausting and just...not her. Plus, she missed the way things used to be, wished they could go back. But his increasing hostility around her had kept her from trying. He snapped at the littlest things, usually directing his frustrations at Krim or Vepar. Poor guys. They took it strangely well, though, didn't seem fazed at all. If that were her and a co-worker, you bet there'd be words!

But today was (hopefully) about furthering the integration of humans and Askari.

The space was immaculate and ready for her guests. Tori donned the *havat*, which she thought fitting, and had agonized over what to serve as food ever since Wells had comm-ed her. She just couldn't bring herself to sacrifice some poor innocent creature alive because that's how they ate their food. So, she'd settled on raw tuna steaks. Because, everyone loved sushi, right?

She met Wells at the door almost as soon as it chimed.

Aderus was with him. As were Krim, Jadar, Vepar and two other Askari she didn't know as well. The big scarred one with the yellow eye was Xaphan. He wasn't too friendly and gave her bad vibes. The other was harder to remember. He was quiet, and she'd not often seen him…Raum?

Tori welcomed them inside with a smile and stood back while Wells lectured about amenities and room designs. He pointed to various areas and Tori had to suppress a snicker at the Askaris' wide, wandering eyes and drawn back ears. They were uncomfortable. And slightly annoyed if their periodic twitching was any indication. Probably because Wells never shut up.

She met Aderus's gaze briefly but forced her eyes away. He had that intense air about him still. The ambassador wanted to show them the adjoining suite and arboretum and Tori voiced that she'd arranged something for them afterward that she hoped they enjoyed. The others started to move away, but Aderus stayed.

"What is there?" He gestured behind her.

"My sleeping quarters," she replied easily, trying not to tense as the others moved off.

"You're going to miss the tour." She nodded toward the retreating group, who were headed into the adjoining suite. Each suite was connected to another, in pairs. They thought it would give the residents their own private space while still feeling close and connected to other Askari.

"Why do you have so many things?"

"I'm sorry?" Tori frowned, a little uneasy he had chosen to stay. And the space was completely free of clutter, the design minimal and modern. "What do you mean?"

"There are many chairs, when you are only one. Platforms with no apparent purpose." He was looking at the sitting area and coffee table.

"That's for guests or when I want to relax. The table is to set food or drink on while I sit. Or whatever else you want."

His snout wrinkled. "Askari like open spaces. When we need something, it is made. When it is not needed, it is unmade."

Tori's brows went up. So, that's why their ship was so sparse! Why she'd seen nothing but empty rooms with the occasional seat or floating table.

"Well, we don't yet have that capability," she reminded him. "Programmable matter. That's impressive."

She watched his tall, lithe form move about the room, reaching out to tap a claw hesitantly against the kitchen counter, as if testing the material.

"I thought much about what you said," he rumbled lowly after a time. So low, she had to struggle to hear him. "And have decided, I am curious and open to your feelings."

Tori had to catch herself. If she were walking, she'd have tripped. The golden-eyed Askari didn't look at her when he spoke and still tapped a claw against the counter.

No. Absolutely not. Not going there. The more time *she'd* had to think about it, the more she was certain she'd made a mistake. Not only had it changed things between them but what had she thought was going to happen? Sex? As if that would be allowed, or more importantly, *possible*? A relationship? She didn't see them as the relationship type.

"I don't—I don't think that's a good idea. In fact, we should forget I ever said anything."

His head jerked up. "You no longer hold interest?"

Tori shifted nervously. "I didn't say that. It's just not something we should, or potentially could, pursue, so I shouldn't have said anything."

A low sound rumbled from his throat. "I struggled to view you in such a way. I could not understand my body's responses and was ashamed of them."

Gee, thanks. Nothing like being told you're an ugly troll by an alien crush to hammer the nail into the coffin. "Well, there ya go. It's a moot point. Let's move on. Why don't we go meet up with the others in the arboretum?" she said, beginning to walk in that direction, but he stepped in front of her.

"You are not what is considered...attractive. Your skin is pallid, your limbs short and bony. You are small and frail and—"

"Yep! I understand. No need to spell it out and no hard feelings," Tori interrupted, trying to move around him. She didn't want to talk about this. But he blocked her moves fluidly and effortlessly.

"Your teeth and nails are dull, your face flat. Your eyes are strange and when you smile, it is—"

"Enough!" she barked, done being insulted and glaring up at him with her "strange" eyes. A part of her was aware how he seemed to feed on her energy. Like he was enjoying provoking her. "I think you'd better leave," she said flatly, refusing to play into it. "These are my quarters and I'm asking you nicely."

His nostrils flared, and his upper lip twitched, but he didn't move. Didn't like that, huh? Well, tough shit. Her patience at an end, Tori raised her hand to usher him toward the door, but he quickly turned the move around on her. In the blink of an eye he was behind her and purred into her ear in dual tones. She felt the heat from his body, but he didn't touch her.

"Looks are not what makes an Askari female attractive. It is their ferocity. You hide it, but it is there, waiting to come out. It is what my body responds to and it makes me start to see past these things. I see them differently because they are you, and I am curious."

Tori's breath caught, and her heart skipped into a frenzied rhythm. She was suddenly on overload. She had never really let herself give in to the feelings before because she knew they weren't smart or mutual and that had kept them in check. But he was practically on top of her now, not as a reaction to some provocation, but because he was interested. In her. In *that* way.

The small flame he had squashed so ruthlessly before roared to life.

Tori swallowed, the weight of it all holding her still. "So. What are you saying?" Her voice sounded breathless and unsure.

She felt a nudge of what she assumed was his jaw against her head. He didn't move otherwise and for a moment they stayed like that. She felt his breath and sensed the tension in his body. Then Tori remembered that, for them, females were the aggressor. Maybe he was waiting for her to make a move? They had turned off the vid feed to her quarters as a courtesy to their guests, but the others could come back at any moment. If she did nothing, though, would he take it as a rejection? Every part of her brain threw up warnings while her body flooded with excitement. With arousal. She didn't want to throw this away. She didn't want to worry about what it would mean or what kind of shit storm would ensue if her superiors found out. She, too, was curious.

By his own admission it was her man-handling that turned him on, so… Tori swallowed and acted on her first impulse, reaching up to fist his locks as before. Aderus hissed and long fingers moved to encircle her neck. Tori gasped. His grip was firm but not painful. The prick of his claws reminded her of their first encounter, but the clicking growl he released in her ear was softer and her breaths quickened. He inhaled, and she felt her core throb. Tori had to try hard to focus. The intensity of her reaction shocked her. She had just meant to give him some sort of indication that she accepted, that she was open to this thing between them. But it couldn't be right now.

"The others could come back at any moment," she warned, licking her lips.

He stiffened behind her. The words had the desired effect, though, and he slowly withdrew. Thank Gaia. Tori didn't know that she had the mental willpower, let alone physical strength, to stop if he kept going.

As if on cue, the door to the adjoining suite chimed. Tori had just enough time to put some space between them and tidy up her appearance. Her heart pounded at the thought they'd somehow know what had been going on, but Wells still chattered away and the other Askari weren't even looking in their direction as they entered her suite.

She tried hard to calm herself as she hurried to the kitchenette and ordered the tuna steaks on the food printer, even smiling at something Wells said and adding to the conversation. She glanced up to catch Aderus's vulturine stare from across the room and quickly looked down to the plates she was preparing, cursing the heat that burned her cheeks.

Lock it up, Victoria!

"I know Askari like live food, but…that's a bit controversial for us," she explained as she rounded the counter, a mask of calm plastered on her face. She set two plates down on the coffee table then turned to retrieve more, catching a horrified look from Wells. He recovered quickly, however, and ushered them to the sitting area. Only Vepar, Aderus and Jadar sat, along with Wells. The other three eyed the chairs warily and chose to stand. She understood the feeling. She was too edgy to sit too. "They're raw tuna steaks," she encouraged when they all just stared dumbly at the plates. "I've tried, uhm, *rukhhal*," she said, stumbling over the pronunciation, "and thought the taste was similar." Six sets of alien eyes, and one human, found her then.

"Well, I choked down a piece," she said sheepishly. "The taste wasn't so much a put-off as the fact it was… alive." Tori paused, clearing her throat. "We prefer not to cause any undue suffering for the animals we consume. And… I suppose that, personally, I don't like to be reminded something is having to die for me to eat." She rambled, as if they needed an explanation.

Someone, maybe Xaphan, made a chuffing noise that sounded mocking. Still, none of them made to try the steaks. Tori fidgeted and was just about to offer them something else when Aderus sliced a small piece with his claw and threw it back. The others watched as his powerful jaw muscles chewed. He said nothing, though, and just as she was about to ask him what he thought, the others looked to their plates and sliced off pieces. Her lips tipped in a small smile and she couldn't help but find his gaze in gratitude.

The visit didn't last much longer. They had made their case and it was now up to the Askari. Tori really hoped some of them chose to integrate onto the *Amendment*, while another part of her worried over the reality of that same outcome. How would they get along living closely with humans? What happened if someone got offended, lashed out, lost their temper? There were going to be loads of misunderstandings. She took a breath. At some point, though, you just had to trust in the bigger picture. Mishaps didn't mean you stopped progress.

Wells thanked her as they exited her quarters. Xaphan gave her a chilling once-over, while Jadar inclined his head in her direction. Tori could hear the ambassador's droning voice start again down the corridor.

Aderus was the last to leave, his golden gaze bright as he stepped up to her.

Gaia, but she did love his eyes.

Tori sensed what she thought was hesitation or frustration. They were feelings she shared but didn't dare say anything, standing as they were to the open corridor.

You need to think seriously on the dangerous, dumb-ass shit you want to do right now... The sensible part of her brain warned.

Fuck being sensible, she fired back, inhaling his scent. Not surprisingly, it was unlike anything she'd come across before, but if she had to label it: smoky with a bite of spice.

Aderus's eyes flared and he drew up straighter.

A sound registered: someone calling him, or that's what she assumed, because after a tense moment, he moved away. Tori watched him leave, battling feelings of relief and disappointment.

"I'll see you tomorrow," she called, in a tone filled with—hopefully not *too* much—enthusiasm, then pressed her lips together. A flick of his ear was the only tell he'd heard her.

Chapter Twenty-Four

Aderus was unsure how to proceed. She had engaged him in her quarters, only to push him away moments later. Though he understood why; they had to be cautious. But the dynamic was completely foreign to him. The uncertainty, the secrecy...the fact she was not his kind. He was still trying to figure out how to read her. And he was one of the more patient among them! Rather than deter him, however, his determination seemed to grow, and he didn't know why. Though, he had an idea. It was the challenge of it that called to him. The thrill of conquering the unknown, of gaining her acceptance. True, she was no match for his physical strength and would be easy to best in breeding, but her strength of will was a different thing. It called to him, pushing him to earn her surrender.

So, it was with a strange, old feeling that he arrived at the airlock the next *sol*. It took him some time to realize that he was excited, even a little anxious, to see her. It was hesitant, tempered, but that was how he felt. And then he remembered why he ruthlessly suppressed such emotions when Wells told them she would not be joining them today and proceeded to try to talk them into a different human coming aboard their vessel.

Did he no longer hold her interest? Had she yet again deceived him? Why did she not come? The ambassador would not elaborate, and it only served to further sour his mood. He was annoyed at the feelings, and more for falling for another possible deception. Had he not learned his lesson the first time?

***

Chickenshit. That's what she was. Tori scrubbed a hand over her face and groaned into the mirror. She'd comm-ed Wells this morning to let him know she didn't feel well and wouldn't be joining them today, when really, she just needed to ball up.

Tori never skipped work; it was her life. The events of the last few weeks only solidified that conviction. She'd been positively giddy with excitement last night...only to have the cold, jarring sting of reality slap her down hard when she thought about what the repercussions might be.

Goddess, but she felt like a mess. Things had sucked lately, but at least she'd known where she stood, at least she'd felt in control again. How was she supposed to act around him now? What were they doing, and where would it lead? She needed to think this through, but that was what had led to her freak-out this morning.

Tori blinked at the pale, wide-eyed woman staring back at her in the mirror and stilled. Was this really who she wanted to be? Someone who worried so much about the "what ifs" that they forgot to live? Forgot how to take chances?

A vision of the last time she'd seen her parents popped into her head, care-free and happy. They had been on their way to the airport, headed to Europe for their first trip abroad...when a Semi swerved and ran them off the road. One minute here, gone the next. And a resounding clarity replaced her frantic thoughts.

The consequences of this choice would be heavy, might even break her, but Tori didn't think she could live with herself if she didn't take it. What was the point of it all, otherwise? Her parents' deaths had at least taught her that much.

So, she comm-ed Wells again around lunchtime, told him she was feeling better and would be going to the gate. Tori didn't really know what she'd do when she got there, but Aderus had told her that her *havat* could communicate with the ship, if ever she needed aboard unannounced. She shouldn't have been surprised when it began to pulse rapidly as she stood outside the exterior airlock, sending waves of warm vibrations through her body. She imagined she must look like one of those jellyfish, standing against the dark, smooth metal of the Askari vessel.

The airlock opened minutes later and Aderus stood facing her.

"Hi," she said softly.

His powerful jaw seemed tense and she noted a guarded look in his eyes. Tori followed him into the chamber, which provided them some privacy, and even knowing that his lack of greeting was normal, it felt cold and critical.

She looked up at him and went for total honesty. "Look. I'm sorry I wasn't here this morning. It wasn't anything you did. I just...I thought too much about everything and got freaked out." She fell quiet a moment. "You make me nervous. I don't know how to act around you now. I don't know how this, should work," she said, gesturing between herself and him. "I just... panicked," she finished, swallowing hard.

He watched her and blinked. "You are female. You initiate."

"Um. Yeah, I don't really know what that means. And what actually happens when you 'respond'? We haven't discussed it. Are you even familiar with how humans have sex? Do we agree that's where this is eventually going to lead?"

A look she'd never seen altered his features and his locks seemed to flatten against his skull as he moved his gaze to the side.

Oh Gaia, I think I embarrassed him!

"Aderus." She frowned and reached out. "I didn't mean to make you uncomfortable." He stiffened and let loose a soft hiss but didn't pull away. She kept her touch light and his black and gold eyes dropped to where she held his hand. "This is new and...awkward...for both of us, but talking about it will only help, I promise."

His laser-focused gaze snapped up to meet hers. "We do not talk about breeding. It is instinctual. It is something that is done." The last words were said with an edge of annoyance. At least, that's the vibe she got. And Tori had learned to rely far more on her other senses when it came to understanding them.

"You're much bigger and stronger than me," she spluttered. "I think you'd understand why I'd want to talk before we do anything!"

"I will not injure you."

Her cheeks flushed as her thoughts flew to exactly *what* they were talking about. "You couldn't know for sure. Not unless we—"

Tori stopped mid-sentence when she realized they weren't alone. Krim stood at the second airlock, Raum hovering behind. She'd been vaguely aware of the creepy crawling sensation as they'd undergone Decon but had been far more focused on the conversation and Aderus. Tori jerked her hand away and felt her cheeks flame as they continued into the vessel. It didn't help that she could feel Krim's and Raum's eyes on her. She didn't know how long they'd been standing there or how much they'd overheard.

She was grateful to round with Jadar. Though Aderus had hissed lowly when she'd smiled at the green-eyed healer in greeting. She finally deduced it was in response to her attention. Whenever it wavered to another Askari for too long, he would do something to bring it back to him. Not too flattering, in her opinion. It reminded her of a spoiled child.

She decided to take a snack break a couple hours later to clear her mind and recharge her batteries. The "common room," as she called it, was the same one in which Aderus had shown her his home and the female hologram. Most of the conversations they'd had had taken place in this room. It was where she went to eat and other Askari rarely entered while she was here. Aderus did say they liked their solitude and didn't tend to eat together, or socialize much, for that matter. She admired the view of the stars from her seat, eating from a container of fruit in her lap.

The corner of her eye caught movement and Tori looked over to find the object of her thoughts standing near the only entrance and exit. Their doors didn't chime so there was no indication of them opening or closing, which was unsettling. One minute you were alone, the next, you had company.

Tori's heart sped up as he came closer. Uncertainty showed in his stance for a moment, but he stayed, staring at her expectantly. Her brows rose, and she quickly finished what she was chewing before setting it to the side and wiping her hands quickly on her thighs. Equal parts gratitude and affection filled her at his actions. This was clearly uncomfortable for him, maybe even taboo, but he had sought her out anyway.

She cleared her throat before speaking and raised her hands in a placating gesture. "I want you to know that I respect how uncomfortable this may be for you. If it helps, um, I'm not too comfortable talking about it either. Not that I don't have experience, but I've always been a bit of an introvert, outside of work."

Tori replayed her words, then quickly added, "Not that I've had a whole lot of experience either. Just the right amount, really." *You sound like a moron.*

His chin lifted. She knew now it usually meant they were scenting the air. "How is it you cycle?"

Tori frowned, confused by his question. "I'm sorry?"

"Female Askari seek to breed when they cycle."

"Oh. Humans…ovulate once a month," she said dumbly, assuming that was the answer he sought.

Aderus grunted at her response. "Come to me then." A dangerous look flashed in his eyes. "Do not approach another Askari." He turned, and it took her a moment to realize he was leaving.

Wait. Why was he leaving? They were about to have an important conversation. Only she realized it was her who'd made that assumption. Apparently, he wasn't interested in conversation. In putting her at ease, at all. No, he just wanted her to come to him when her biology dictated she'd be "in the mood." Like a bitch in heat. And then what? Keep your mouth shut and drop your pants?

Un-fucking-believable!

She'd given serious thought to respecting his boundaries. He said he wouldn't hurt her and the thought of just winging it and trusting him held major appeal. It was exhilarating and sexy and scary, all at the same time. But any thoughts of intimacy ground to a halt at the cold, uncaring picture he painted. Like two animals scratching an itch.

"Hey!" She bolted from the chair and met him before he reached the door. "For your information, humans may ovulate once a month, but we can, and do, *breed* whenever we're in the mood. We don't have to cycle. Which you can forget about now, since you don't even care enough to talk about something I feel is important for us."

His eyes flashed down at her and she could sense the change in him. Tori knew her outburst was initiating the exact opposite of what she said (which was all other kinds of effed-up), but Goddess dammit, why was he making this so difficult? She could admit she was judging him by human standards, and that was unfair, but it was all she had to go on.

"What is important?" he prodded.

"Ugh! Don't play dumb. You know what I'm talking about."

Tori paused. She could practically feel the anticipation coming off him in waves. Had this been his intention all along? To get her riled up into coming after him again in a fit of passion? His breathing was up, she noticed, as was her own, and a look of challenge showed in his eyes. It wasn't the first time, she realized.

Well, two can play that game.

Tori took a deliberate step closer; it put them easily within touching distance. His intensity faltered a fraction.

"On Earth, females *or* males can initiate, so you're going to have to meet me halfway," she said smartly, then stopped as a thought hit her. "In fact, consider it a challenge."

His body language changed then. The large Askari's eyes brightened, and his clawed fingers twitched at his sides. He drew up straighter and his tresses puffed out.

"Come to my quarters, on the *Amendment*, and I'll promise no talking."

She had him. He'd have to approach Wells, come up with a reason. He'd have to go outside his comfort zone. If there was one thing she'd learned working with them, it was that Askari were more stubborn than any human she'd ever met.

Tori drew her hands behind her back and rose up onto her toes, then back down with a shit-eating grin. Yup, it felt good to call the shots, she thought.

Now maybe they could have an honest-to-goodness adult conversation!

Chapter Twenty-Five

Earthers had no respect for instinct, no understanding that some things were not meant to be analyzed to death by words. She wanted to talk...about breeding, about human sex. But Aderus couldn't bring himself to do it. What if what he told her, she didn't like? What if she told him something that made him question the act? Or himself? Or her acceptance of him? Already, he had done far more for her than he'd ever done for any other, and she wasn't even his kind!

Now she challenged him. Whereas an Askari would have done so simply, physically, she challenged him in deed and with words. Humans. They were always over-thinking (or over-speaking), absorbed and obsessed with their feelings and expectations of the same in others. It was exhausting.

He would not do it, he thought, as he listened to Vepar relay the condition of their drives. Others were present, too, any that had pertinent knowledge and/or skill: Braxas, Krim, Sallos and Jinn. Aderus was there so he could know and communicate what they needed.

If it was meant to be, it would happen so, he decided, his thoughts turning unwillingly back to her. Earning a female's trust and approval was part of the act, and if accepting her challenge saved him talking about it, then his choice was clear. Just the idea had him feeling anxious, when he'd never worried over breeding before. It happened, it was sometimes satisfying.

Silence drew his attention back. The others were looking at him.

"You stand gawping like one of them," Braxas rumbled.

The male's hellish experiences had earned him some small allowances, but Aderus still curled his lip in warning. "I will communicate our needs to the *khurzha,* and their ambassador."

"She has no power to get us what we need," he growled. "She is a healer, which we no longer need."

Aderus stiffened, a soft hiss escaping his throat. The male was bigger than him, the deformities he suffered adding to his bulk. Aderus studied him carefully. His stance was easy, his words were snide (perhaps to vent frustration and dislike of anything alien anywhere near him), but they were not meant to provoke. He was stating his mind.

"She is the reason you live," he reminded him keenly. "I will go talk, I will get what we need."

"I will go, too," Krim voiced.

"And I," Jinn said, drawing his gaze.

***

"I did, but intake is being flooded with requests right now, not to mention security. It's like a twelve-month wait just for the background check."

Tori was eating dinner as she chatted with Liv on a vid call. "Yeah, but I put in a good word for you. Hopefully that will help speed things along," she mouthed around her hand as she chewed (Mom had always been a stickler for etiquette).

Having Liv here with her would be so great. She missed her friend, and with the room designs of the new wing, she and Liv could have connecting suites. It'd be like their college days: sharing meals, watching movies, talking shit until one a.m. Well, maybe more like eleven. Tori needed her beauty rest. Getting older sucked.

"How is work going?" she asked.

"Meh. Same old. People got problems, I have a job. The day we turn into robots, now that's when I'll be in trouble."

Tori smiled, then grew serious. "You know, they're going to be a lot more difficult than probably anyone you've ever worked with, but I think it's a great idea. All of them were imprisoned, some were tortured. I wouldn't be surprised if the concept doesn't exist to them, but therapy could be beneficial. At the very least it'd prepare them better to interact with humans. What do you call it, emotional conditioning?"

"Don't get my hopes up, but yes, emotional sensitivity training." Liv nodded. "They'd have to approve the proposal first."

The door chimed in the middle of her next bite. "Who's that?"

Tori frowned. "Don't know. I'm not expecting anyone." She'd already showered and changed into her comfy clothes.

"Mmm, company." Liv wagged her eyebrows.

"Yeah, right," Tori said dryly as she set her bowl down and pulled up the feed to the outer corridor next to Liv's smirking face.

Tori's smile dropped. It was Aderus and two other Askari. But where was Wells? Why hadn't he comm-ed to let her know they'd be coming? Her words from earlier played through her mind. She'd been bluffing, but he hadn't known that. She quickly tamped down her panic. It looked like Krim and someone else were with him. Definitely not a personal call.

"What? Who is it? I can see from here, you're white as a sheet," she heard Liv say.

"It's them."

Liv's eyes widened. "Don't disconnect! Please? I want to see them! It probably has to do with some exciting top-secret shit."

"You know I can't do that. I'll call you later." Tori ended the call to the sound of Liv's protests.

She tried to act calm as she went to the door. Liv was right; it obviously had to do with something important.

"Hey! This is a surprise. What's going on? Is everything okay?" she rambled in greeting, then stepped aside to allow them to enter, waving off their escorts.

"What do you wear?" Aderus asked, raking her with a strange look.

"Oh, uh, these are my lounge clothes." His eyes flicked to her *havat*, the small round disc still attached at the base of her neck. He had seen her in little else since the day he'd given it to her, but this was different; she was off-duty and relaxing in her quarters. "What's going on? No one told me you were coming. Is everything okay?" she repeated, genuinely concerned.

"We came to discuss our needs with your ambassador. He said he had to meet with Earth governments right away. Jinn and Krim wanted to see human quarters."

"Oh. That's great!" Tori glanced around him to Krim and the newcomer. His light violet eyes jogged her memory, as did the way he wore his *havat,* covering nearly every visible inch of skin. She'd seen him maybe once or twice in passing on their vessel. Another quiet one. Or rather, she hadn't had the occasion to speak to him.

Tori tried not to seem too excited, but this was a really good sign. These two could be the first to integrate onto the *Amendment*.

"In that case, look around. Krim, I know you're familiar, but feel free to show Jinn the adjoining suite and arboretum." She smiled in greeting at the violet-eyed male. "Are any of you hungry?"

"No," Krim and Aderus rumbled in unison.

Oh-kay. That's a clear no on the tuna.

"Excuse me one sec," she said, slipping toward her bedroom. Her top fell to just above her knees and the thick, cotton stockings covered her thighs, but pants were far more appropriate, given her unexpected guests.

Tori hurried to the linen closet next to the en suite and grabbed some scrub bottoms.

"Does your *havat* not function?"

She hadn't realized someone followed her until he spoke, and she startled at the deep dual tones.

"Good Goddess! What are you doing? Where are Krim and Jinn?" Her heart jumped at the distinctly intimate scene.

Aderus took another step into the room and his chin lifted as his eyes roamed. Her smell would be strongest here.

"They are exploring. Testing your food generators."

"Oh. Okay. You can't just come in here, though."

His gaze shot to hers. "You told me to come."

Shit. She was hoping he'd forgotten. Her nerves spiked. "I did, but...we can't do anything."

He tensed. "You issued challenge but do not honor it?"

"W-what are you saying?" she stumbled. "That you want to throw down right here? Seriously?" She waved her arm that still held the scrub bottoms.

"I did not say. I met your challenge," he replied. "Is that not what Earth *men* do?"

She blinked at him. The timing was horrible, with the other two only rooms away, but her patience had reached a breaking point with the constant back and forth. Deciding she'd gone a little crazy, Tori walked up to him.

"You want to know what Earth men do?" She kept eye contact and reached out to lift his clawed hand gently over her left breast.

She held her breath, waiting for his reaction.

The dark Askari stiffened and his lip twitched. His hand sat motionless under hers. The moment grew, became awkward; he didn't seem into it at all. If anything, he was trying to avoid touching her with his fingers.

Tori stepped back at the surprising prick of tears. "See? This is what I mean. We don't even know what—" She broke off and looked away with a self-derisive snort. "And you don't seem to care. You just want me to attack you like an animal, jump on you and tear you to shreds, like that—"

She'd been rambling in frustration but blinked up at the low rumble that sounded. His eyes burned into her now, and it looked like he was restraining himself from coming closer. It was like her words had flipped a switch and there was no denying his interest. The fact it ignited an answering spark in her both thrilled and annoyed her.

She studied him. "That's what you want, isn't it? Why you like to goad me. Don't think I haven't noticed."

His chin tipped up again. "It is what you want, too, I think."

Her eyes widened in surprise, then her jaw tightened. "What I want is to be able to talk about things before we fumble into them. But maybe that's where I'm going wrong with you."

Tori couldn't believe she was acting on the impulse as she spoke aloud to the room's computer, the command enclosing them in the privacy of her bedroom. She grabbed his hand again and held it to her while the other reached up to firmly fist his tresses, a move she knew excited him. She had accused him of being uncompromising, when maybe it was her who was refusing to give. If he wanted action and she wanted words, then maybe the answer was to combine the two. Tori nearly trembled but managed a small smile when he crowded her with a clicking growl.

"How about, I'll show you something and you show me something," she said softly.

His irises flamed. This felt good, it felt right, she thought, looking down. Her fingers were small and pale next to his, his claws resting lightly above her collarbone. When she nudged his hand under hers, the nipple hardened, and her back arched on a sharp inhale. On her toes, as she was, the move tightened her grip and Aderus hissed, then spun her around. Or had he moved behind her? Either way, Tori blinked at the abrupt change in position.

Long fingers framed her jaw in a hold that was as unsettling as it was familiar, and his other arm wrapped around her torso. He chuffed and nuzzled her hair, his grip tightening like he was expecting a fight. And Goddess help her, it turned her on. Tori squirmed. She wanted to touch him, wanted him to touch her.

"Aderus..." She halted when she felt him sniff her neck, the act both crude and sensual. Giving up on getting free, she grasped the part of his arm she could reach, trying to communicate what she needed. "Put your hand where it was before," she demanded, pressing her (much duller) nails into the back of his neck, trying to get him to do her bidding.

She gasped when he dropped them both to the floor on their knees instead, and his grip tightened with a rumble in her ear. He loomed over her, one dark hand braced on the floor. She stilled, growing confused. Was he purposely hindering her efforts to participate? Tori turned her face into his.

"You're going to have to touch me, you know, if you want this to go anywhere."

After some hesitation, a clawed hand jerked up to her chest, and Tori almost laughed at the rough, clumsy way he handled her.

"Like this," she said gently, and carefully moved his hand under her sweater and on top of her breast. She suppressed a moan when his textured skin brushed her nipple over the thin cotton bra, and her breath quickened. "Right there," she coaxed, and moved his fingers lightly over the tip. One of his fingers twitched, then she felt him move without her guidance. Her head fell forward as the feeling shot straight to her clit. Tori couldn't ever remember getting this turned on by some light petting, but almost everything about the dark Askari seemed to affect her strongly. Her hips rolled back, and she felt him tighten his hold again with a clicking growl.

"I'm not fighting you. It feels good," she breathed. Goddess, everything about this felt amazing. It didn't matter they were different, that it could be dangerous, and that they had no idea what they were doing. Tori wanted him.

"Sit me up so I can take off my top," she demanded, pushing back against him. He stilled, and she could sense his uncertainty. Tori decided she was going to have to find out exactly how Askari *bred*. But that would mean she was already thinking about a next time and that'd be getting way ahead of things... Instead, she lifted her head and turned it back toward him again, inhaling his unique scent and snuggling his jaw. "Please." The move was a more intimate version of what he'd done to her.

Aderus jerked, and for a moment Tori feared she'd done something he didn't like, but then he yanked her upright with him.

She scrambled to remove the sweater in the process, which proved difficult when he didn't want to release her. "You're going to have to..." She gasped when the material ripped, and he wrapped both arms around her.

An urge hit her hard then. She wanted to see them. Wanted to see the vision they painted of coal and cream and his wraithlike eyes.

Tori spoke aloud to the ship's computer and the display panel on the wall across the room gave way to a mirror. She could just see them in it, where they knelt on the floor. The top of her head barely reached his collarbone and long arms banded her stomach and chest. He nuzzled and sniffed her head again as his eyes looked down her body. The stockings had slipped low on her thighs, black bikini briefs covered her pussy, and he must have caught her bra with the sweater because it hung in pieces between them. One breast was bare, jutting out from between his arms, nipple hard and seeking attention. Her cheeks flushed at the lewd scene, but it sent her arousal soaring and Tori whimpered with need. She could feel how wet she was.

A part of her worried what she was getting herself into. She knew she should be more cautious about all of this...but she trusted him. There it was. And he had said he wouldn't harm her, so she assumed he was similar enough to a human man in that regard. It was common knowledge they'd hacked most of Earth's databases upon arrival, so it wasn't like he hadn't had the opportunity to look into it.

"I need your hand again," she breathed, not able to use more direct words with him yet. Her head rolled to the side, against his chest, and she realized he was still wearing his *havat*.

The thought of him against her, completely naked, skin to skin, was a little intimidating and she couldn't help a nervous tremble. But her want and curiosity were far greater than anything else.

Tori nudged the material with her cheek. "And take this off," she murmured, at the same time she decided she was done being docile. Her arms lay trapped at her sides, but that didn't mean she couldn't touch him. Tori boldly reached back to run her hand up his thigh, but Aderus hissed and jerked his hips away. Two rows of dagger-like teeth flashed in warning and she froze, confused and a little hurt. Then a vision of the holo-pic female filled her mind. Maybe pleasurable caresses weren't high on their list of familiars.

She swallowed and reached back again but paused at his clicking growl. "I'd never hurt you, Aderus. I only want to touch you. It's important for humans. I really liked it when you touched me." She watched him in the mirror as his head lifted, found their reflection and stilled, taking it in. Tori wondered if what he saw excited him as much as it did her. His fiery gaze held hers as she reached back again. His nostrils flared with his breaths. Tori was panting, too. She felt slowly up his thigh. He was incredibly tense behind her, but his clawed fingers moved closer to her exposed breast, tracking her movements.

Her eyes closed as his textured skin brushed the tip. "Goddess," she moaned.

Her hand slipped the rest of the way to cup his crotch. His lips curled back, and he thrust his teeth against her throat with a guttural growl, as if to say, "play nice," as he watched her from beneath his prominent brow. But she had no intention of harming him, and the thought that sex had perhaps been painful for him in any way made her ache to bring him pleasure. The bulge she felt was big, but she didn't feel any of the "usual" defining features. Tori started to worry as she carefully caressed him. His breaths puffed against her jaw, blowing her hair, which had long since come undone from its messy bun. The growling stopped, and she felt the tension in his muscles lessen. She kept her touches gentle but insistent and eventually his lips dropped to cover those shark-like teeth. His fingers twitched over her nipple and the ensuing zing of pleasure pushed past her inhibitions.

"Don't stop, that feels amazing." She turned and crooned into his ear. On impulse, she licked him. Tori openly admitted she was obsessed with their long, pointed ears that sometimes moved with their emotions. Aderus snarled and fell back onto his haunches, bringing her with him.

His hard bulge pressed against her backside as she sat in his lap, legs splayed awkwardly over his thighs, but none of that mattered when what felt like wet bristles grazed her neck. She tensed in surprise, at both the reciprocal lick and the sensation that sent goosebumps racing down her body. Her hands found whatever part of him they could then, but he still wore the damn alien leotard.

"Take it off," she complained, panting. He didn't move at first, but then one arm released her to reach under his locks, and the material retracted, uncovering his body to her hungry gaze. Tori was only half aware of what she was doing as she placed small, urgent kisses along his jaw, her senses on overload. He tensed and clicked at her in warning but quickly relaxed when he saw she meant no harm. "I'd never do anything to hurt you," she repeated, meeting his fierce eyes.

Tori was so caught up in the feel of his skin that the wet, thick thing against her backside didn't register at first. Her eyes had fluttered closed and she arched into him, humming her pleasure. It was so much better than she imagined it'd be. She felt a gush from her pussy and inhaled sharply. Tori had never been so turned on in her life. She could feel her heartbeat in her clit.

The poke of something at the edge of her panties made her take stock, though. It was wet and hard and felt as if it was trying to get inside. She jumped with a squeak, her eyes flying open to meet his in the mirror as his hold tightened.

"What in the Hell was that?" Tori tried not to sound panicked but failed. His claws curled into her skin and the thing moving below her stilled. He growled low.

"My *pvost*. It seeks you."

"What do you mean, 'it seeks me'? That's *you*, right?"

A pause. "Yes."

"I don't know about this," she yelped and jumped a second time when it brushed against her panties again, drawing her legs up on top of his. "It's like it has a mind of its own. Human men's...er...*pvosts* don't do that," she bit out.

His body grew rigid behind her and his irises contracted. "I trusted your words to me."

"Right." Tori licked her lips, holding his gaze. "Just...take it really, really slow, okay?" Tori couldn't help the anxiety that clawed its way up her body. She tried to relax, to get back into it, but that was a lot easier said than done. She wasn't going to suggest she take the panties off either, not until she knew what she was dealing with. Call her one-sided, but he didn't have to deal with a part of her anatomy going *inside* him. Her gaze stayed glued to the mirror, focused on their lower halves.

Aderus rumbled into her neck, the arm around her tightening and shelving her breasts. His heavy tresses fell forward, brushing her nipples, and she swallowed hard, cursing the throbbing between her legs. The prodding at her panties became more insistent and Tori's breath came quicker. Aderus buried his face in her hair a little roughly and moved his long fingers to frame her jaw again. The hold made it hard to move. His *pvost* found its way under the fabric and Tori jerked. Then a soft, pretty sound started in her ear. It reminded her of the sound she'd heard from the crimson-eyed male, back when she gave him her blood. A purring hum. "What's happening?"

"Remain still," he panted.

His sounds against her back sent vibrations down her front. Goddess help her, but she was still turned on something fierce. Alien dick and all. Maybe it was those differences that she found so exciting. She felt her core clench and didn't want to admit that the thing moving in her panties had anything to do with it. Tori watched, enthralled, trying to catch a glimpse, but couldn't see much so she focused on the feel. It was moist, hard, and...flexible. A good size, too. Her breath caught, and she tensed when it found her slit. It slicked slowly up along her cleft, until it nudged her clit and Tori jolted, crying out.

Aderus's grip on her jaw tightened and he hissed, obviously misunderstanding what was happening.

"Again!" she barked, past concern, as her nails dug hard into his thighs and she met his molten gaze in the mirror. She wiggled impatiently, trying to get him where she needed him. A slip, another nudge, and Tori moaned her pleasure loudly, throwing her hips back against him. His irises narrowed, studying her movements, and after a long pause, he repeated the motion hesitantly; once, twice, she lost count. "Yes, just like that," she encouraged.

Tori closed her eyes and rode his slippery appendage, waves of pleasure crashing through her, building quickly. The purring resumed, his movements growing more certain, as an arm pulled their lower halves flush. Her gaze found their reflection again and she pulled at her panties, jerking them to the side. She wanted to see it, wanted to see them together. His *pvost* was lighter in color than the rest of him, and it glistened as it surged between her lips. Gaia, he was much larger than anyone she'd ever been with. Tori swallowed. It seemed to move independently of Aderus, too, which kind of freaked her out, but also filled her head with possibilities. It was tapered at the tip, not rounded, and had to be pretty long if it reached her clit from behind. Tori felt Aderus's hips move behind her, slightly out of rhythm. She let herself drown in what he was doing to her as her gaze devoured the picture they painted: her nipples peeking through his tresses, hooked claws framing her face, her breasts jutting over his arm as his *pvost* slicked through her folds, bumping her clit. His bright gold gaze found hers just then, and it was too much. Tori's eyes went wide as her orgasm hit her. Her muscles locked, and she cried out.

Aderus froze again, growling, but she slapped his thigh. "In me! In me!" was all she could manage as her core bore down on nothing. She wanted to weep in frustration, then in relief as she felt something prodding her entrance. She heard hissing and clicking, her hips still bucking with release, but she couldn't help it.

"Hurry! *Now*," she sobbed. "Aderus, I need—" Dark fingers covered her mouth, smothering her pleas, at the same time his *pvost* finally breached her entrance. Her eyes went wide as he filled her, stretched her. She could feel how tight she was from her release. The intense sensation, combined with the erotic act of his hand over her mouth, sent her into another orgasm.

***

Aderus hissed viciously and tried not to panic as her channel strangled him. He hadn't really known what to expect, had struggled to keep up with her demands and reactions. The little *khurzha* didn't thrash or bite at him, as a fierce female would. Instead, she encouraged his advances and seemed to relish petting and rubbing. She grabbed at him with urgency, but not to cause harm, and Aderus was shocked to realize he had let his guard down more than once. It enabled him to lose himself in the act in a way he never had before, which incited his arousal to a surprising degree.

Dread and alarm seized at him now, however, as her channel bore down on the most vulnerable part of him. At least, with an Askari female, one only had to get past her teeth and claws. Once inside, her body posed no threat. Apparently, it was the opposite with humans. And *she* had worried about *him* hurting *her*?!

Aderus had listened to her when she ordered him to breach her and now look where he was. His heart raced as he held still, only a slight tremor betraying him. He curled his claws into her soft flesh and watched their reflection. Tori seemed lost to the sensations wracking her body, her pale neck exposed, eyes closed. To fight her or to try to tear out of her now might cause more damage to his person, so he held still, dreading what came next. Aderus jerked when her channel began to pulsate and ripple around him. The ensuing wave of pleasure/pain overwhelmed him, and he snarled into her mane, the light, wispy tresses puffing with his breaths. Tori made a low, keening sound around his fingers and pushed back against him. Her hips pumped him in little movements as her channel continued its rhythmic contractions and Aderus lowered his head and swallowed.

Her posture softened, her movements no longer jerky. But instead of snarling and snapping him away from her, she melted back against him, undulating on his *pvost* as if she owned it. His eyes widened as a different sensation overtook him.

An arm broke free in his distraction and she reached into his tresses, brushing his ear. Aderus *krhuned* loudly as his *pvost* surged in release. Despite knowing better, his eyes closed, and his jaw locked as an intense feeling flowed from his center, almost stabbing.

Their size difference meant he had tried to be careful and move slowly. Still, the end of her channel was not hard to find, and his body sought the entrance to her womb of its own accord. His mind might know that the act was fruitless, but his *pvost* seemed to rejoice as it circled and caressed her inside.

Tori squirmed in his arms, trying to speak through his fingers, but Aderus was overwhelmed by sensation. He started when he felt his *pvost* filling again, though. He realized she hadn't made to separate herself from him. An Askari female would turn on him as soon as she felt she had tolerated all she cared to, but Tori gave him no such indication. So, his body would continue to breed her.

His hips moved again, he couldn't control it, and he buried his face against her mane, deciding to give himself over to her.

Chapter Twenty-Six

A fleeting feeling of alarm washed over her, only to be drowned out by the pleasure of his thick member working inside the confines of her spent pussy. Tori felt something drip down the inside of her thigh, so she assumed he'd come. Though, it might be her own juices, considering how hard she orgasmed. She was incredibly tight and a little tender, but the feeling was out of this world when he started to move inside her again. Actually, it felt like he'd never stopped, and Tori swallowed and closed her eyes, willing to take every last drop of pleasure he could give. A quick glimpse at their reflection showed he still seemed to be into it, so she pushed her hips back onto him.

He dropped his head and click-growled into her neck as his movements became harsher. Tori inhaled sharply. It didn't take long, and she was right on the edge again. Part of her marveled at how quickly he'd gotten her there, but then, she had little experience with multiple orgasms. As the moments passed, however, she realized she'd need something more to push her over. Tori fumbled for her clit with her fingers, his arm around her tightening as he hissed, apparently not liking the movement. But she needed to come and didn't have the patience or mental capacity to explain it to him. So she moaned and bit down firmly on his hand.

The purring stopped with a series of clicks and he stilled. Tori used the opportunity to reach her hand toward her center, but he was quicker, releasing her mouth to wrap his fingers almost painfully around her wrist, jerking it out to the side.

His eyes met hers in the mirror: confused, concerned, accusing. The last threw her. Tori's eyes widened as she felt him begin to withdraw. "No! Don't! I just need more," she rush-whispered through panting breaths. Her voice sounded raspy. Probably from all the noise she'd been making.

"Let go of my hand and watch. I'll only touch myself." His eyes didn't leave hers in their reflection, and the gold narrowed ever so slightly. After a moment, he released her, and Tori moved to touch herself. She licked her lips and widened her thighs over his. Aderus dropped his gaze, focusing on her movements with unnerving intensity. Tori kept expecting to feel embarrassed by the act, but as she watched him, watching her, it only fed her arousal. Her channel throbbed and twitched around his girth, made beyond slick by their juices, and she sighed as she worked herself on him in small pumps. The lewd noises their bodies made barely registered. Goddess, it felt so good! This is exactly what she'd needed, she thought, as her fingers circled her clit more firmly. She tried to keep her movements to a minimum, that she'd startled him, but the sharp twinges of pleasure soon built, and her breath caught as she felt the impending crash upon her. Tori jerked when she felt Aderus's long fingers ghost past her own, to gently explore where they were joined, and it threw her hurtling over the edge.

A low wail was torn from her throat before she bit her lip to silence herself. She barely knew who she was in that moment; so intense, it was scary. Her muscles locked so that she couldn't move, and her channel clamped down on him like a vise. She was vaguely aware of Aderus clicking into her ear as she felt them lurch forward. An arm banded her chest and hips, holding her suspended, claws digging painfully into the flesh of her hip. No sooner had her pussy relented its grip than the large Askari fucked her in rough, shallow strokes. Tori's eyes widened. Had she thought what she just felt was intense? Holy Mother Gaia! Oh, Jezus!

She slammed her eyes closed and whimpered, doing her best to ride out the storm. What he was doing to her felt so good, it bordered on painful. Her head rose, seeking their reflection. Aderus looked like some wild thing. Snarling and hissing, his face tucked against the top of her head. Not for the first time, alarm dampened her lust, but Tori refused to feel fear. Her eyes fluttered closed as she forced away any negative emotion and surrendered to him. Her body went lax, which only seemed to excite him more, and the pleasure overwhelmed her, and he continued to draw out her orgasm.

His movements stuttered, and he stiffened, then Tori felt the hot wash of his release a moment later. She moaned at the lingering contractions of her muscles around him and breathed sharply when she felt movement. She thought she'd imagined it before, but no. There was a suction and tickle at her cervix as he continued to flood her, wetness seeping down her thighs. They were joined together so closely that Tori couldn't move as he ground against her ass with tight, urgent motions. She felt him root against her neck and shoulder, pushing her head to the side.

Their harsh, panting breaths filled the space and she didn't even flinch when a clawed hand slammed down on the floor next to her. He rasped something in Askari that she wished she had the strength to question, but he'd fucked her senseless. Her knees thudded, leaving only the arm banding her chest keeping her from kissing the floor. She was completely boneless, unable to move. He slid most of the way out of her and she winced at the burn. It was probably the most sex she'd had in...ever, but throw in his size and intensity and no doubt, she was going to be sore for a while. Tori lifted her hand to grip the forearm holding her.

"That was—I don't." Damn, she couldn't even find words.

A soft chime interrupted, indicating someone was outside the bedroom. Tori didn't even respond at first, her brain not functioning fully. But a bolt of panic hit when the fog suddenly cleared.

"Krim and Jinn!"

The walls were almost completely soundproof, so she was certain they wouldn't have heard much, but it still did not look good. Tori scrambled away from him and launched herself at the linen closet, stumbling and trying to shove her limbs into the first thing she grabbed. She threw a frantic look over her shoulder at her Askari lover as he pulled himself to his full height, watching her, and froze as her eyes moved over his form. His heavy tresses hung loose about his shoulders and her gaze caught on the rough patches of skin down his neck, across his chest and along his arms and legs. She'd felt the scrape of them more than once. The tips of his claws hung level with his knees and his powerful heels arched high above the floor. Something about his anatomy reminded her of the ancient beasts of Earth, raw and powerful.

Tori blinked. She thought him beautiful. Even his appendage-less groin, which was a complete shock and had her obsessing over where his *pvost* had come from, didn't alter that fact, she realized. Maybe it was because he'd just given her the best sex of her life, but she couldn't even think of a human man right now. The thought scared her, and she turned away from him to wipe quickly with a rag and step into a new pair of scrub bottoms.

"This is *not* good. Get dressed! They can't know what happened."

"They will know," he said with a sniff, as the *havat* flowed down to cover his body.

Tori swore. Their scent. She wasn't a perfume person, but there was scented moisturizer somewhere. She spotted it on the nightstand, snatching her torn clothes from the floor on the way and shoving them under the mattress. The chime sounded again.

She squirted a generous amount on her hands and began to rub furiously at her neck, arms and face. Aderus watched her, nose wrinkling.

"Here," she said, advancing on him with a handful, but he grabbed her wrist with a hiss.

"Now you smell like breeding and bad plants."

Tori moaned in frustration. "Aderus! We need to try to hide what happened. I've no doubt they'll find out eventually, but I need some time to figure out how to handle this with my superiors. There's no telling—"

An annoyed chuff sounded. "You insult our intelligence. Even Askari who resent our situation would not do anything to endanger their own lives, if they thought Earth would react badly."

Tori gaped. He had a point.

The day ended with them all sitting silently in the common area for an hour or so until Wells had finally shown up. Krim and Jinn had done nothing but stare after she and Aderus came out of her bedroom. Jinn had moved back, while Krim tracked her every move, as she donned a fake smile and slipped past them into the kitchenette to grab a drink. She refused to feel ashamed and Aderus's little speech had put her mind at ease, for now, but assurances didn't fix awkward.

"Anyone thirsty?" she'd asked in a pleasant tone.

When no one responded, she'd filled two cups with water and brought one over to Aderus. He'd been having a riveting visual discussion with the other two but met her gaze when she handed him the glass. He took it, gaze flicking tentatively to the chair next to him. Tori raised her brows and sat down, quietly sipping her water until Wells came.

Later that night, once she'd let herself think, however, she couldn't stop.

When she'd given herself permission to throw caution to the wind, it was with the reasoning that whatever happened would be a one-time thing. It had to be, and she got the impression Aderus wouldn't know anything else. But what if he approached her again?

Tori wouldn't have the strength to turn him down, she knew that now.

She chewed her lip. What would that mean for her career? Her feelings? Because she *had* developed feelings for him, she realized, and reluctantly admitted the only person she felt closer to was Liv, and that was because they'd known one another for years. Liv knew her mind, inside and out, but Aderus... What had happened between them had been intense and Tori knew without a doubt she felt intimately closer to him than any other person she'd ever been with, and he wasn't even human.

The yearning to know him, to learn everything about him that she possibly could, clawed at her.

And she didn't even know the details of his man parts!

Tori frowned. Had he enjoyed it? Of course, he did—he'd come, hadn't he? She'd watched him a lot during and he *seemed* to enjoy it. Tori rubbed her face and sighed loudly, ending with a groan, then flopped onto her stomach and ordered herself to sleep.

Chapter Twenty-Seven

By now, most of the others scented what he'd done. Xaphan looked him down in disgust, while Braxas had hissed away from him. Most did not know what to think of it, though there were a few interested sniffs. He found those annoyed him the most and knew it was because if Tori were Askari, they would be in competition. But she was not, which he found oddly freeing. And deeply unsettling.

The things he'd felt with her...why had he not felt them during any other breeding? That a female not of his species should be the one to elicit such intensity of feeling seemed...wrong somehow.

Aderus had but to think of her—caged in his arms, fighting to pet him, milking his *pvost*—and said organ stirred, his *vryll* awakening in delight. The answer came to him then. No Askari female would allow a male anything else, save fighting, tooth and claw, for his right to mount her. Breeding was not about feeling. It was about instinct and strong offspring.

His claws clicked in thought. Earthers approached it differently. Their instinct to breed seemed to be driven by pleasure. Now he understood what she meant when she said they didn't have to cycle. Tori could seek to breed again, whenever and as often as she felt.

Aderus halted and flicked his ears. If so, *he* wanted to be the one she chose.

He asked Jadar and Raum to join him the next *sol* at the gate to the Earth vessel. Tori seemed subdued as she stepped into the chamber with him, her gaze downcast. Jadar looked at him, noticing as well. Her *havat* covered more of her skin, and Aderus sniffed the air but did not scent anything unusual.

He stood next to her through the sterilization process and twitched his fingers in offer, almost without realizing. A surprising contented feeling stole through him when her small hand wrapped around them.

She looked up at him, smiling briefly. "I'll be in the common room today for mid meal if you'd like to join me." He didn't respond but fully intended to accept the offer. He just refused to give those listening any more information about their dalliances.

He left her to discuss medical things with Jadar but stayed near enough. The danger was increased, as his mind obsessed over the reactions of the others.

Around midday, she broke off and he followed. She looked up from her food when he entered, delicate brows rising in surprise. "Oh, I didn't know if you'd come, but I'm glad."

She seemed more relaxed now and he wondered if something had happened before. He went to the generator for some *rukhhal* and sat down across from her, hunching over his food.

He looked up when she made a sound in the back of her throat. "So. What kinds of things do you like to do for fun? What do you enjoy?"

He thought, chewing vigorously. "Killing *Maekhurz*. *Rukhhal*." He grunted, then paused. "Breeding you."

Her face contorted as she choked on a piece of food. "Well, that answers that question. I was wondering if you'd—I did, too." Her cheeks reddened, signaling she was uncomfortable, though he didn't understand why.

"A lot, actually," she added softly. "But I meant more along the lines of hobbies. For instance, I like to read, play chess..."

"What is chess?"

"It's a game of strategy. You try to beat your opponent by taking away their players, and eventually, their lead piece, called a king."

"Warring."

Tori pursed her lips. "I suppose you're right. It's a game, though, no one actually dies."

He grunted. "Younglings play games." His mind traced back to those times. "I enjoyed the cliffs."

"Cliffs?"

He studied her, debating the conversation. "Askara is mountainous, much bigger than on Earth. I roamed them as a youngling. Hunting *dahvhrin*."

"What's that?"

Aderus was surprised at his sudden enthusiasm to talk about something he hadn't thought of for many *sols*. "*Dahvhrin* live on the cliffs, their tresses blend with the rock. Fast and deadly; they know you are there before you ever see them. Solitary creatures, revered on Askara, but sometimes they reveal themselves. Their tresses glow and they will come to you, if they sense you are worthy."

Tori's mouth hung open. "Come to you? To do what?"

"Befriend a fellow *shktal*. Strong spirit."

"And did one ever reveal themselves to you?"

Aderus couldn't help the pleased trill that sounded in his throat. "Twice."

Tori smiled, her blue and white eyes sparkling. "Aderus, that's amazing. I wish I could have seen it. We can definitely add *dahvhrin* hunting to the list of things you enjoy, I think."

He shifted restlessly. It felt...uncomfortably intimate, voicing such things.

"I petted a tiger once, when I was little." Her eyes grew unfocused. "It's a big, deadly predator. My dad's friend worked at the zoo and he snuck us in while they were fixing a tooth. He was anesthetized." Her gaze fluttered back to his. "I've always thought the most dangerous things are also the most beautiful."

Silence stretched between them and the air stirred. Aderus stilled and stopped eating. "You are needing," he hissed softly, knowing the scent now.

Tori squirmed in her seat. "Excuse me?" Her expression hinted she knew what he meant.

His eyes tracked her every movement, nostrils flaring. "Why did you not come to me?"

Tori put aside her own food. "What do you mean? It's not like I was walking around *ready to go* earlier. You just do that to me sometimes." She seemed flustered. It roused his interest more.

"No others make you need?"

"What? No!" She looked offended now. "You're the only one, of *you*, I feel that way toward. And I'm not a slave to my sex drive. I can control myself. Just because I may want to doesn't mean I will, or should."

"Why not?" She was confusing.

"Because." The *khurzha* shifted in her seat again. "I didn't think you'd want to. And, it's dangerous. I think that if we do it again I'll...want something I can't have."

Her words made no sense and Aderus tensed as he felt himself respond. The pull to her was strong, likely because his body knew what to expect. And unlike her, he honored his instincts. They were telling him she needed breeding; his whole being clamored with anticipation. A female Askari would have advanced on him by now.

"Will you come to me or not?" he questioned, ears pushing forward. His eyes hunted over her as she stood, lifting her arms in the air. He stood, too.

"Really? Before, Krim and Jinn were next door. Now, anyone could walk in. I know they rarely do, but still. And I told you, humans do things differently. Just because I'm aroused doesn't mean I have to have sex. Don't you put this all on me: equal opportunity, remember?"

She stared at him, expectantly, something heavy in her gaze. Then she turned away with a chuff. "Right, yeah," she mumbled, lips tight and eyes shining. Tori stepped past him to grab her food things.

Aderus advanced on her, roughly burying his snout in her tresses with a growled hiss. Her face showed surprise, but it was what she had been trying to communicate, he was sure. A part of him waited for her to beat him away, but her needing scent was strong and he could hear her breaths, felt the fast beats of her heart. He was less certain of the touches she had shown him, as his claws dragged over the flesh of her backside. He waited, hoping she would engage him.

"Oh, Good Reason, fuck it." She said breathlessly.

Aderus braced himself when she seized his nape with blunt fingers, climbing his body. Their position was wrong, but he wouldn't risk refusing her. Her hand found the bulge at his groin and he clicked low, baring his teeth, then blinked when she mouthed along his jaw.

"Retract your *havat*, just the bottom. Someone could walk in," she panted. He bristled at her demanding tone, craved it. Her legs wrapped his middle, supporting her weight, which he barely felt. So similar, but different. Perhaps it was why she felt so good inside.

His *vryll* trembled at her persistent petting and his *pvost* shifted with impatience. His breaths quickened at the thought of seeking her tight, soft, channel. Tori looked down as she touched him.

"What are you waiting for?"

Aderus felt his tresses flatten. He'd never been uncomfortable about his body, but she would see all of him in this position and he remembered how she had reacted before.

"Aderus? Hey."

Her blue and white eyes locked with his and she moved her hand to his face. "If you're worried, don't be. I want to see you."

She grasped one of his hands and tugged it to her rear, while the one on his face slipped under his mane. She was feeling for the disc of his *havat*, he realized. His nostrils flared as he willed it to respond. Tori held his gaze then looked down as it receded up his legs and groin. He let his *vryll* part, then started and snarled at the light touch of her fingers, knocking them away.

"I want to feel you, please?" Her eyes were wide, lips parted.

His body had closed in reflex, but when she reached for him again, his *vryll* parted as if by command. He remained tense as she gently explored him, his breaths harsh. She petted his folds and his *pvost* moved forward as if seeking the attention. Tori gasped, pulling back only slightly, but her fingers came back to him, determined. Aderus tightened his hold on her and growled against her mane when her digits circled his length, moving over him in a sort of dance. No one had ever touched him like it before and his body's response was swift and brutal. He grabbed at her fine tresses, pulling her head back, and hissed as he felt for her *havat* with his thumb. His *pvost* was already prodding against the covering between her legs, searching for her entrance.

Tori panted, eyes heavy. "Wait, I wanted to—" She broke off with a noise when he acted on the impulse to tongue her neck. Aderus remembered from before that it seemed to excite her, and he sought her taste.

Her needing scent grew stronger as the *havat* uncovered her lower half and he felt small fingers grasp his back. His *pvost* sought her entrance, almost as soon as it was revealed, and Tori groaned, her head dropping forward onto his chest with harsh breaths as he breached her. Aderus grit his teeth. She felt smaller than before, and he fought to fill her then loosed a low clicking growl, walking them to the wall. He felt her mouth along his jaw again as he bred her with tempered, eager pushes.

Aderus faltered when the little *khurzha* mouthed his lips. It was strange, and he pulled away, but she was insistent, grabbing his chin and doing it again. He chuffed in annoyance, breaking her hold again, but stilled at a smooth, wet lick against his lip. His *pvost* surged in response and Tori made a noise, gripping him even harder. Her little tongue slipped into his mouth to glide along his teeth and Aderus jerked.

He inhaled sharply.

A familiar taste blossomed on his tongue and started him *krhuning*, pushing into her with more urgency as his tongue licked toward her, seeking more. Suddenly he felt loose and fierce, heat and strength, bliss and restlessness.

Aderus dropped and bred her in hard, unrestrained strokes. Tori yelled and tore her head to the side, her body locking around him, then clenching in waves, and Aderus grunted at the pleasure/pain it brought, huffing into her shoulder and letting it bring forth his seed.

Afterward, he blinked against her skin, amazed at the tremble in his limbs. Tori was lax against him, their chests moving with their breaths. He shifted, rumbling at the squeeze to his *pvost*. Aderus looked down, a part of him still expecting her to beat him back from her and noticed marks along her skin. His claw brushed the area and Tori squirmed.

"That tickles," she said, following his gaze. "Just a few scrapes and bruises. Not like I didn't expect it, tangling with you."

His ears pulled back. "You wear your *havat* differently."

"Yeah, because I'm losing sleep over what's going to happen when they find out." Her easy manner fell, and she pushed at his chest, his *pvost* slipping from her body. He felt the air thicken.

"Most humans have sex as part of a relationship, Aderus." She spoke softly and watched him intently. "Do Askari have those? Pair bonds?"

"We pair to breed." It was what they just did. Why was she asking him about it?

"Do males and females form relationships outside of that, though? You know: live together, care for each other?"

He hissed at the idea. No female would tolerate a male living with her and no male would want to. Sickly or disabled individuals sometimes chose to share space for mutual advantage, but no healthy Askari wanted that. Aderus knew humans lived in groups called families. "Askari are solitary," he rumbled.

"I see," she said, looking away. "We can't do this again."

A shift in the air drew his attention and he tensed with a low clicking growl. Tori gasped and tumbled behind him when she realized the cause: the *palkriv* had entered and stood watching them.

Aderus slowly found his feet, gaze trained on the male. He felt for his *havat* and covered himself, but didn't move, waiting to see how the intruder acted. Various emotions hinted across his unfavorable features and calculating stare. Aderus had never heard of a female choosing a *palkriv*, though he supposed it could happen, if one made it to adulthood. The male's eyes repeatedly sought Tori, and Aderus hissed, drawing his attention back. Her safety was his responsibility and this one had almost cost them their lives. Aderus admired strength, but didn't like him, and showed it.

Tense moments passed. With one last glance toward her, the male turned and left. Aderus huffed and eased his stance, looking back. She had donned her *havat* and the flesh of her face lacked even more color than usual.

"I can't believe that just happened." Her words were low and mumbled but grew in volume as she became more upset.

"We had it coming, though. I mean, what the—never mind. I'm so embarrassed. Could you walk me back, please? I think I'm done for the day."

Aderus did so but felt distracted and annoyed. Tori was distressed, but he'd been interrupted during breeding before, it was not that uncommon. Sometimes the intruder challenged. Sometimes the female threw you for him. But when the *palkriv* entered, he had felt a deeper indignation. Perhaps it was because he had fought him once already. Or because he didn't like the way he looked at the little *khurzha*, like they shared something that the rest of them, Aderus included, did not.

He considered what she'd said. These things were entirely dependent on the female, so he didn't understand why she felt the need to tell him it could not happen again. Still, he couldn't deny the satisfaction of knowing that he was the only one that appealed to her. That when she felt the need again, he would be the one she sought. This was the "relationship" she spoke of, he was sure. The concept was new and strange, but Aderus understood the attraction now. He had only bred the same female twice, that he could remember, and no past experience stood out from the rest. No matter how much it might unsettle him, she did. A small, frail creature not even his kind.

She hadn't even looked at the *palkriv*, he thought with pride. She'd hidden behind him, which wasn't very becoming of a fierce female, but he supposed he'd rather have her sole attentions. Most males were greedy that way.

He knew she feared how her people were going to act when it was found what they had done. But Aderus sensed they already knew.

He was imprisoned for many *sols*, knew what it felt like to be watched by technology far more advanced than what humans possessed. It had taken time for him to realize the feeling for what it was, and by then his body had already begun to respond to her. It had deterred him, at first, but dealing with his emotions had been more of a struggle. Braxas and Jinn had made some progress, so their vessel was not quite as vulnerable as before. They could maneuver farther from Earth, should the need arise, but they had an alliance with the humans now that supplied them with materials and, soon, vessels. None of them would risk the opportunity to fight back, even if it was with the aid of an unknown world.

A dark feeling stole over him as they approached the gate, and his ears drew back. While she agonized over the would-be reactions of her people, Aderus's suspicion grew. She seemed to think their response would be harsh. Yet they knew, and did nothing. Which meant they wanted something, or they were waiting. Either way, he knew it looked better for her if she did not know, so he did not tell her.

Tori turned to him at the gate. His body blocked Raum from view and the airlock had not yet opened. Her eyes were bright and shiny as she grabbed his hand with both of hers. He stiffened, surprised by the gesture. "I wish that things were different. I'll see you tomorrow, okay? Goodbye, Aderus."

An overwhelming feeling of unease stole over him that perplexed him. He didn't want her to go back to her ship, but there was no reason he could name. Aderus watched her go, dwelling on if he had ignored his instincts again to their detriment.

Chapter Twenty-Eight

Tori comm-ed that she was returning early because she wasn't feeling well. She knew it was more mental than physiological, with what had just happened, but dutifully followed quarantine procedures. She felt drained, extremely tired. Maybe she *was* coming down with something, after all.

She was led to a clean room off the Med Ward where Menez checked her over and took some blood, all suited up, per safety protocols. She'd had to draw the blood herself, courtesy of Henry and his protective impulses. She lay down on a small cot while she waited for someone to come debrief her. She'd slept in rooms like these almost more than her own quarters when duty called.

Tori woke with a start what felt like minutes later. She was in the fetal position, in agony. Her skin was burning hot, but she shook with the chills and her *havat* was slick with sweat. There was someone in the room with her. A nurse?

"What's going on? How long have I been out?" Her voice sounded dry and raspy.

"Just try to relax, Doctor. Everything is going to be fine."

"Everything is *not* fine. It feels like I'm being gutted." She winced, moaning in pain. Her eyes blinked open and focused on a white biohazard suit. The person in the room with her was covered head to toe. Oh, this was not good. Dread made her head pound. Or maybe that was the fever.

The nurse came closer, trying to calm her. But he stopped, a strange look on his face.

"What? What is it?" That look scared her almost more than the pain.

He didn't say anything, just backed away from her, his gaze frozen.

"What in the hell is it?!" she repeated, struggling to control her panic, and rolled to face the two-way mirror along the wall. Her heart skipped. For a moment she was paralyzed. Then Tori struggled to her feet, amid his protests, and hobbled closer, one arm banding her midsection.

Blue irises glittered and sparkled like jewels in the light; black rings surrounded them, stark against her whites and bleeding into the center. The eyes blinking back at her were not her own. At least, not the ones she had always known.

More importantly, they weren't human.

Author's Note

Beloved Readers,

Wow. I sincerely hope you enjoyed Tori and Aderus's story, which is concluded in Part II, *Chasing Earth*. As my first book, I know it's far from perfect and hope you'll be gentle with me, as I'm certainly open to constructive feedback. Old Harlequins started my love affair with romance when I was a teenager, but it wasn't until I discovered paranormal romance that I really found my passion. This truly is a dream come true and I'm *so* excited to delve more into the world of the Askari. I hope you are, too! Yes, this is intended as a series, and there will be more books (Braxas, Krim, Jadar, the *palkriv*—known as Tannin, we'll find out).

There were two big themes in this first story that I tried really hard to stick to: 1) That aliens should be aliens. Their appearance, their mannerisms, their culture. And I tried really hard to portray that. I felt an instant attraction wouldn't be realistic and would take time to grow. 2) The political, social and psychological considerations. Hence, a 100,000-word HEA (with Parts I and II). I do not plan the other books in the series to be as long, as we get a lot of the preliminaries out of the way with Tori and Aderus's story. If you felt the romance lacking in *Saving Askara*, I can tell you, Part II will be more focused on developing that aspect.

I'd love to hear from you! Connect with me on Facebook (JMLinkAuthor), Twitter (@linktojm) or my blog https://jm-linkblog.blogspot.com. I'll be posting releases and promos on my blog, so subscribe for emails. And if you liked Part I, please, please leave a review ;)

Love and Hugs. Dream on.

JM

ALSO BY J.M. LINK:
<u>ASKARI SERIES</u>
SAVING ASKARA (TORI & ADERUS BOOK 1)
CHASING EARTH (TORI & ADERUS BOOK 2)
SPANNING WORLDS (MINA & JADAR)
<u>FAE VEIL SERIES</u>
WHEN FAE COLLIDE

AUDIOBOOKS
SAVING ASKARA, narrated by Keira Stevens
CHASING EARTH, narrated by Keira Stevens *coming soon!*